I0676767

Georgia Cowboy

Charlie Barnett

Copyright © 2012 Charlie Barnett / Gateswood Press

All rights reserved. No part of this book may be reproduced or transmitted in any form or by any means, graphic, electronic, or mechanical, including photocopying, recording, taping, or by any information storage retrieval system, without the permission in writing from the publisher.

Book cover design by Melvin Barnett

ISBN: 978-0615589367

Printed In the United States of America

Dedication

I would like to take this opportunity to acknowledge two dear friends that have passed away during the time this book was being written: My father, Charlie Sr. and Otis Gulledge, a dear friend. I spoke at both their funerals. They both will be missed very much, not only by me, but everyone who knew them.

Contents

Acknowledgments

I am extremely grateful for the help and support of the following:

First to God, for blessing me with the incredible gift of life, and for divinely guiding me on my own journey into His will of ministry, and my hobby as writing.

To my darling wife, Janice, who has always encouraged me in every venture I have taken, for the past fifty-three years.

To my four sons: Montie, Michael, Melvin, Matthew. These guys have made me proud to be their father. From the day they were born they have shown me respect beyond measure, which at times I didn't deserve.

Could I say this very proudly? Just as the wife and I, my four boys have never been divorced...thanks to my daughters-in-law. I love you guys very much, also.

Chapter One

I guess seeing any young man still wearing the gray uniform, after the Battle of the Blue and Gray, was enough to make a sane man go wrong back in those days. Many had lost a loved one, and some their sense of direction and pride. Just losing the war for the South was a stumbling block. Bill Allen had lost it all.

He was only nineteen as he stood a couple of inches above six feet. He was thin in the waist and hips, but wide across his shoulders, where it mattered most. Hard muscle bulged under the sleeves of his washed-out denim shirt and his hands were big and scarred from fighting a little over two years for the Confederacy. His army issue boots were much scarred and down-at-the-heel. His eyes were hazel, but showed more ice green than brown when anger was upon him, as it was now. Bill stood in the front yard of his old home place with very mixed emotions. He was leaning back against the picket fence gate, the only thing left standing after the Atlanta fire. He began to reminisce how as a child playing with his dog Spot he would watch his ma use the brush-broom sweeping up every sprig of grass in the yard. "Its time to start dinner, honey child" she would say, "Pa will be coming out of the field now dreckly'. Our ol' black, three-legged wash pot was lying on its side in the back yard, close to where the smokehouse once stood. Pa's gambling-stick survived the fire, still hanging on a tree limb out side the picket fence that once stood.

"Good to see'ya back home, Mr. Bill," a familiar voice came from out of nowhere. I quickly spun around, seeing a black man coming from out of the bushes. "Is that you, Ham?" I asked with a loud tone. "Yes sir, I hid myself when I seed'ya come riding up. I didn't know who you is."

"Well it's me, Ham...what's left after two years of fighting and killing." Ham and I hugged necks and shook hands.

"Mr. Bill, I sure am sorry about yo folks, and the ol' home place. The missus has got a pot of turnips on cooking down at the shack. If you would, come on down and we'll talk a spell."

"Ham, my old friend, you know how I love your wife's turnip greens and her pone of corn bread. Why I can't count the times as a boy I stuck my feet under your table." Ham was looking up in the sky, smiling from ear to ear, reminiscing of old times before the war. "I'll bet she pitched a chunk of dead hog in them turnips to make your tongue slap your tonsils."

"Hush yo mouth boy, my mouth done started watering just thinking about that pot of greens." His eyes glistened and nearly formed a tear.

"Thanks anyway, Ham, I just don't feel like eating or talking much right now. I done got too much on my plate already. I think I'm gonna head west." I took my boot and moved around a little sand. "There's really nothing around here for me anymore. Maybe I just need to get off and find myself." And with nothing more than the clothes on Bill's back and a service revolver hung low on his hip, he mounted his faithful horse Buddy, and rode off into the sunset.

Bill wasn't in any hurry to get anywhere, and no one was waiting on him if he did get to where he was going. He left the state of Georgia pulling an attitude a city block long, and a chip on his shoulder that would weigh any grown man down. His future plans for his life were detained by a useless war. His marriage plans were crushed by an unfaithful woman and a first cousin he never liked to begin with, and his inheritance was a pile of ashes south of Atlanta.

Bill was living off the land; about the only thing he had left to love was fishing and hunting. The rivers and creeks supplied his every need as he rode across the state of Alabama, although it broke his heart to see the huge plantation homes in ruin and the bare cotton fields. It was early one beautiful evening, some place in central Alabama, when Bill decided to cool off his saddle and give Buddy a rest. Bill found the perfect spot to spend the night. To Buddy's liking there were gobs of some luscious green grass mixed with wild clover. Now Buddy could get caught up on his grazing. Bill took the saddle off Buddy and began to curry him down. Buddy lost no time as he began to nibble. But what really caught Bill's eye was a stream not more than a rock's throw, just a few yards away. It was a still running creek with deep black fishing holes.

While he was catching supper, Bill tied Buddy with a long rope so he wouldn't wander off and get lost. Crickets were plentiful under the bark of a large lightning-struck pine that the wind had blown down. Bill had already strung up four hand-sized bream and was getting another bite when two men came riding up on the same horse. It was noticeable to Bill that the two riding double were eyeballing his horse. He also noticed them eyeing the gun hanging low on his side. In my way of thinking, they figured he just might be a gunslinger and nobody was gonna pull the wool over his eyes.

"Having any luck young fellow?" the man sitting in the saddle asked. Bill smiled, "Got enough for supper." The two continued on down the road out of sight. Now I know I'm not the sharpest knife in the drawer, but I ain't stupid either. I haven't seen the last of these two men, Bill thought. I went ahead and enjoyed my supper and built up a small bonfire for the night. Buddy was still chomping grass like there was no tomorrow. I had my saddle for a pillow and made my bed, using pine straw to form a fake body, while I took my place in the bushes just a few steps away. I kept my ear trained, and my eye pealed, mostly cat-napping. The camp fire was almost burned down, and just as I had thought, I heard a twig snap. 'Course in the dead of night it sounded like a bass drum. The two men had come slipping back. I watched the two silhouettes slowly make their way into my camp intending to steal my horse. I watched while one ghostly shadow eased over and held my horse while the other came creeping up to my bed with his pistol in his hand.

"I wouldn't shoot my blankets full of holes, mister," I said, surprising the intruder. He wheeled and fired a shot where he thought I was, I heard the hot lead whiz by my head. As I pulled the trigger on my Navy Colt, a streak of fire and hot lead reached his body with a striking sound. He folded up like a cheap accordion and hit the ground near the fire with a thud like a toe sack full of Idaho spuds. The man that was holding my horse had less brains than I thought. He turned loose of Buddy and began running my way, firing his pistol in the dark. With four shots left in my equalizer, I cut him down like a pesky weed in a garden fence row. With my pistol still cocked and smoking, I eased out of my hiding place to check the two bodies. Just as I thought, I had shot them both through the heart.

Now dead men lying around don't bother me none in the least. I had seen many in the war in my few years in battle. It's just something about these two that gave me the willies. I thought, I'll just move my bed until morning, and that I did. I was up early the next morning and saddled Buddy and sniffed me a good lung full of cool air. I mounted up and began to look for their horse. I soon caught up with their mount and went back where the two men were lying. Can you believe it? They hadn't moved a muscle during the long night.

Now I want you to know, I'm not in a habit of stealing from the dead, but I didn't figure they'd mind much if I borrowed their new looking Henry rifle. As I stood there admiring the workmanship of this fine repeating long gun, I thought, I'm gonna surely need a place to keep it on my horse, and I politely relieved them of their saddle holster as well. I didn't have one, you know. Well, I might as well use their saddle bags also, they will come in handy. As I started to transfer the saddle bags from their horse to my horse, they sure are full of something, I thought. It wasn't my place to haul their dirty laundry around with me, so I unbuckled the two straps. Now what I saw wasn't long-handles or dirty socks. I was surprised, to say the least. I thought to my self, Bill Allen, your ship has just come in. I quickly opened the other saddle bag; it was stuffed just as full of big bills as the first. And to ice the cake this was Yankee money, good as gold, and would spend anywhere.

My first, second, and third thought were all the same, these two men were bank robbers, and I'll bet most anything they run one of their horses to death getting away from a posse. Well, at least I could starve the buzzards and bury the bodies, but I don't have a shovel, I quickly thought. I rolled the men up in their blankets and tied them across the horse, hoping for a town up ahead or the loan of a shovel soon. I guess I had ridden about two hours when I spied a farm house up ahead. I thought, I'll kill two birds with one stone, I needed a swig of water and I know the horses were about done in, also.

It was a scorching hot day in late August. At least I could get water and borrow a shovel. I was about a hundred yards from the farm house when I heard a shot ring out. Well, I certainly don't need my hair parted this morning. I heard the chunk whiz by. It missed me by a mile, but I don't like folks shooting at me. "Don't you come any closer, mister," came a somewhat distressful voice from the old house. "The next time I won't miss." Well, my mama didn't raise any fools, so I stopped dead in my tracks.

"What do you want, mister?" the voice cried out again.

"I just want to get some water and borrow a shovel to bury these two men!" I yelled back.

"Who are the two men?" the voice replied.

"I don't know, they were trying to steal my horse last night so I shot 'em."

"Are you a sheriff?" came the voice. "Come on up a little closer so I can see who you are." I could tell it was a girl's voice, and no telling what she might do next.

"No! I ain't no sheriff, I'm Bill Allen from Atlanta. I'm headed out west to strike gold and get rich, and you need to put that smoke pole down before you shoot yourself in the foot."

"You just better mind your mouth, mister. I can shoot a squirrel out of the tallest pine tree in this here state." The door, such as it was, began to ease open.

"Can I get off my horse? My rump needs a cooling off."

"I guess you can…if you are who you say you are." I kept my eyes fixed on the front door until the young girl came out on the porch. She leaned the flintlock relic beside the wall and started down the ragged steps. Now I don't mind telling you she was a sight to behold. She was barefooted as a yard dog, and her hair hadn't seen a comb in weeks.

"You ain't gonna try nothing funny, are ya?" she asked. Placing her hands on her hips and arching her back, she began to look me over. I took one more look and quickly made a rash decision.

"Young lady, I don't know where your mind is, but rest assured there will be no shenanigans going on around here this morning."

"Well… my ma warned me many times about strange men, and what they might do."

"Your ma was right young lady, but she wasn't talking about me. Is your ma in the house?"

"No! My ma is dead, she died last year."

"I'm sorry to hear that. Is your pa around?"

"No, he left to fight, and I heard he got killed, and that's been nearly three years ago." I began stretching my neck looking all around.

"Who's keeping the farm up? Looks like you have everything in order." I said, walking up a little closer to her.

"You are looking at her. I do all the work by myself."

"Do you have a name, and a shovel that I might borrow?"

"Yes, I have two shovels, and my name is Mary Brooks, but everyone just calls me Mary, for short; you can too, if you want to." She slightly lowered her head and started moving sand around with her big toe. "Come on down to the barn, or what's left of it. A twister last Spring wanted the back part, and I ain't fixed it yet."

I could see what she was referring to as she and I approached the barn. "I keep all the tools down here." I could sense she liked animals. I watched as she patted my horse in a loving way. "If you want to, Mr. Bill, you can unsaddle your horse and put him in that make shift corral over there." She then eased over to a side room on the old barn. "I got plenty of corn. You can give him a nubbin or two. He looks a little thin in the mid section."

"Now that's right neighborly of you, he hasn't had anything but grass in a week of Sundays." She cocked her head to one side, shrugged her shoulders and caught my gaze.

"Now just because I'm being neighborly, don't you get any funny ideas," she said in a soft, blushing tone.

"No Ma'am, not a funny idea crossed my mind, and I want to thank you for the loan of the shovel, too."

"I can tell you right off, Mr. Bill, there is some easy digging over behind that forty, that's where I buried mama." She pointed to a field behind the barn.

"I tell you what I think I'll do since I ain't busy right now this minute. I'm gonna give you a hand digging the graves." She took a step over to the horse. "I was just thinking you might consider giving me the dead men's horse, seeing that they won't be needing it no more!" she exclaimed, inspecting the two shovels. "You take the shovel with the long handle and I'll use the short handled shovel." She slung her hair to one side. "I tell you what else I'm gonna do, Mr. Bill, when we finish planting these two fellows, I'm gonna fix us a good supper, well that is if you ain't tried nothing funny by then."

"You can rest assured, Miss Mary, there ain't a funny bone in my whole body as I know of."

"You know, mister, I been doing me some thinking here lately, Mama might not have been right about everything she told me, you reckon?" I took me one more look at her, she hadn't washed in a week, and if she pulled off that filthy dress it would have followed her around.

"You best mind your mama. She is right on everything she's told you. Besides, I been doing me some thinking, too. You know, Mary... these two men were bank robbers...and you might not want to bury them down here with your mama." I never will forget the way she looked at me. "Well for crying out loud, Mr. Bill, she ain't gonna know it." As I stuck the shovel in the ground I was thinking, she ain't as dumb as I first thought.

"I guess you've got a point, and this is easy digging. I don't see any reason you can't have their horse. And you might as well have their gun rigging. They have some good looking revolvers." In less time than it would take to tell it, she and I were heading back to the house. I was toting the shovels and she was leading the horse.

Chapter Two

"I wonder what the horse's name is?" she asked, rubbing her cheek against the horse's muzzle.

"Since it is your horse, you can name him anything you want to. It ain't gonna make him mad. Do you even know how to ride a horse?" She looked me all over, and pouted out her lips... "Yes! We had a horse. Pa rode him off to the war, and I guess some damn Yankee killed him, too." Mary changed her course and started toward a garden up a ways from the house.

"What do you think about fresh fried rabbit for supper?"

"That sounds good to me. Do you know where we might come up with a rabbit?"

"I shore do, look over there!" she said as she pointed. I looked over at the end of a row of turnips and there sat a trap, with two rabbits in it, hopping around trying to free themselves.

"Did you make this trap?" I asked, giving it the ol' eagle eye.

"I shore did," she said with a big smile.

"This is neat. I can see you are very handy with your hands." This statement seemed to break the ice.

"I'm a good cook, too; my ma and pa taught me well before they died. I just wish I could read and write. My folks never went to school neither." She walked over close to me and handed me the reins of her horse. "Iffen you will go by the barn and unsaddle my horse, and pitch him a nubbin or two, I'll take care of these rabbits for our supper."

I did as she asked and unsaddled the horse, penning him with my horse, and put the shovels back where they belonged. She ain't much, I thought, but for a minute she made me forget about the war and my problem.

As I started to the house I stopped by the well where there was a long trough full of water, and thought I would wash my shirt. It was soaking wet with sweat to begin with. I raised my arm and smelled an odor I could do without. The way the sun was beating down, I figured if I gave the shirt a good squeezing it would be dry before supper. As I was hanging my shirt on a rail fence that ran parallel to the house, I saw a lone rider coming toward the house. With nothing more to do, I stood my ground and waited for the man to ride up.

"Good evening, sir." I said, propping up on the fence.

"Well, it was a good evening, but it's got a little sour, I suppose," I looked all around. I thought he was talking about the weather; it did look like we might have a chance for an evening shower. "I've been on the trail of two bank robbers, but lost their tracks early this morning, after a gully washer a good ways back."

"I don't see a badge, you must be a bounty hunter," I replied.

"You got me pegged right, young fellow, and I always get my man. Do you mind if I water my horse while we're jawing?"

"Help yourself, there is a bucket and dipper of fresh water sitting on the well curb." He slid out of the saddle and led his horse over to the trough. While his horse was getting filled, he gave the dipper a try.

"You say you are trailing two men that robbed a bank, but lost their tracks due to a down pour?" He wiped his mouth on the back of his sleeve, and reached for the reins of his horse.

"That's about the size of it. I been tailing them for over a week and they have given me the slip two or three times. I'm about ready to give up on 'em." I thought to myself, that would be the smart thing to do if I were you, but said nothing.

"I thought I would just ask around the community, somebody might have seen 'em, and I might pick up their track again."

"Well, I sure wished I could help you, mister, but I ain't seen hair nor hide of these bank robbers; by the way, was there a reward out for these men?" I asked.

"It sure was, five hundred dollars…and I wouldn't be wasting my time. Well good day to you, son, and thanks for the water." I stood and watched as he rode out of sight, hoping that would be the last I would ever see of this bounty hunter. My shirt was still damp as I eased on to the house, hoping I might hang it on a chair near the stove to finish drying out. The front door was sprawled wide open so I looked all around... an went on in.

"It will be ready in just a minute," Mary said, turning around smiling at me. I hung my shirt on the back of a chair and pulled it near the wood stove. "How about checking the biscuits in the oven to see if they are brown yet. I don't want the rabbit to burn." I could tell this wasn't Mary's first rodeo, she knew how to cook. I opened the oven and there sat a pan full of golden brown, big, cat-head biscuits, that would tempt any man. What was that old saying about the way to a man's heart was through his stomach?

There, sitting on the edge of the stove, was a platter of fried rabbit that made my mouth start watering. "Now, if you would, get us a couple of cups out of the cabinet and set them on the table for our coffee. I set the tin of biscuits on the table and got the cups. "Go ahead and smear a little cow butter on all the biscuits; you will find it already sitting on the table."

I pinched myself on my bare arm to see if this was all real. For a few seconds more I had forgotten all about the war and all that killing, and dead bodies lying all around me. I even forgot about my girl friend who ran off to Pensacola with my first cousin.

"Go ahead and sit down," Mary said, as she set the platter of beautiful fried rabbit on the table between us. Then she sat down. "Would you like to say grace over our food?' she asked.

"Would you please go ahead. I don't do a good blessing." She smiled and bowed her head. "Lord, thank You for the food, and just keep right on sending those rabbits, and thank You for sending someone by to share it with, Amen." I waited to see if she was going to use a knife or fork, but soon saw she was behind the door when manners come calling. So without further ado, I did the same.

"This is the best fried rabbit I have ever tasted!" I exclaimed. She caught my gaze and smiled. "And these biscuits are light as a feather."

"Well, eat all you want, we'll have the rest in the morning with some fried eggs and grits," Mary replied, with a rabbit leg in one hand and a biscuit in the other.

"I've been meaning to ask you, is there a town with a general store near by?" She laid her half eaten rabbit leg on the table, wiped her greasy hand on the front of her dress, and took a big slug of her black coffee.

"Yes, there is, and it's not too far from here, right on up the road out there. You thinking about needing to go, are you?"

"Well, yes, there are a few things I'm in need of, and thought I would pick up for my trip out west."

"You still thinkin' about going out west, are you?" I got the feeling she wanted me to hang around.

"Yes I am, just got my heart set on it. You know what they say, the grass is greener over the hill, and a rolling stone don't gather no moss." She cocked her head and shrugged her shoulders. "No, I don't believe I've ever heard that. But do you know what today is?" We had finished eating and just sat at the table talking.

"No, is it your birthday?" She smiled all over herself.

"No! It's Saturday. I'm gonna take a bath and change my dress before we go to bed. You see that tub of hot water settin' over behind the stove?" I thought, it ain't a day too early either, but said nothing. "Are you going to wash and comb your hair, as well?"

"I'll probably wash my hair, but I can't comb it."

"I'm sorry to hear that, do you have tender scalp?"

"No! The dad-burn dog chewed up the comb before he died."

"I have a comb and a finger nail kit and a bar of good smelling soap in my saddle bag over there. I bought it in Atlanta before I left the city. Do you mind if I trim your finger and toe nails real nice after you take your bath?"

"You gonna let me use your soap, are you? I haven't had any soap since Mama died." It looked like it, but I kept my mouth shut for now. Mary took the bar of good smelling soap from me and laid it on the edge of the wood stove close to the number three wash tub filled with warm water.

Oh no, you don't reckon…while the thought was still in my head she started pulling off her dress. I quickly turned my head, "Do you mind if I start a fire in the fire place in the living room? It will give me light to trim your finger nails. And besides, it will take the chill out of the air." I went on in the living room and sat on the floor in front of the big fire place as I started the fire. I had the fire roaring by the time Mary finished taking her bath.

There was nothing left to my imagination as Mary came in the living room to finish drying her hair…Oh, she had on a dress, but standing in front of the fire her silhouette was a beautifully shaped body.

"Sit down with me, and I will comb all the knots out of your hair." Without any hesitation she sat down and scooted right up between my legs. I began to comb her long and, what could be, silky hair. I began trying to remove the kinks and knots without hurting her. This was nearly impossible, but I did it, thanks to the little scissors that came in the kit. "Now that I am finished go look in the mirror, you have beautiful hair now," I said, trying to lift her up.

"But we don't have one, when the twister came throw back in the spring it fell off the wall and broke all to smithereens."

"Well, never mind, here's one in this little leather case." She took it from me and rolled over closer to the fire place. She lay there for the longest, turning the mirror up and down. I don't mind saying going out west, or to town tomorrow, was far from my mind

"Do you think I'm pretty?" she asked, holding the leather case to her chest. looking my way. At first I didn't quite know what to say. I didn't know if I said yes if she would think I was coming on to her, and I didn't want to be fresh or forward. I was actually enjoying her company. You might say she had actually helped me find myself. Just tell the truth, I thought, and let the chips fall where they will is the best policy.

"Yes, I do, you are a very beautiful girl, and so smart too." She didn't say anything but rolled back over laying her head on my leg. "Will you...be my friend? You know, just thinking back, Mr. Bill, I haven't had a friend since Mama died last year."

"Mary, I'm near about scared to say yes, I'm near about scared to say I'll be your friend, because every friend I claim - he or she dies or something bad happens."

"I know just what you mean, Mr. Bill, take my dog for instance, and look what happened to him." My curiosity got the best of me, and I had to ask. "What happened to your dog?" Mary moved around a bit. Her head now lying in my lap, she looked right straight up in my eyes.

"Well, just north of here is a cave or an old mine shaft, nearly grown up it is, but the opening still remains. Now Spot, that was my dog's name, he was a rather large dog and loved to chase squirrels and rabbits. He also had a habit of running into the cave and barking, and watching the leather-winged bats fly out. Oh well, back during early summer I was up there picking blackberries when Spot dashed into the cave and went to barking as always. I could tell it wasn't normal, only a few bats flew out and began to circle the mouth of the cave. 'Course I didn't give it no never mind and started on back home. This is when I heard Spot, the tone of his bark was not the same; he began to squeal and almost cry out that he was in trouble. Well, I didn't know what to do; I sure wasn't going in that cave. Well, in less time than it would take to tell it, out of that cave here he came with his hair all rustled up and his tongue hanging out nearly touching the ground. I could tell something had bit him all over, especially his face and nose, his nose was a sight, and a big chunk was missing. By the time he and I got home his face had begun to swell. I felt so sorry for him, but I still didn't know what to do. I even dabbed some horse-lineament on him. I could tell right off Spot rejected it, it must have burned his nose. It did keep the flies off his face for a while." She stopped her story and sat up right in front of me.

"Is that it? What happened to Spot, did he get well or what?" Mary took the little leather case with all the grooming tools and handed it to me. "I thought you were going to trim my finger nails," she stated, holding her arm and hand up in front of me.

"I am! I am, but what happened to your dog, Spot?"

"I was up early the next morning, course the sun was up, and he was still lying on the end of the front porch. Some of the swelling has gone down but he acted very strange; he actually snapped at me twice as I raked out some food in front of him. Spot never did this before... this is when I saw him foaming at the mouth."

"I'm not hurting you, am I?" I asked. As I cut her broken and jagged nails I saw her cuticles and finger nails were dirty and in a mess. "Go on about the dog foaming at the mouth." I saw I wasn't hurting her, and Mary seemed to be loving her free manicure.

"This wasn't the first time I had seen this happen, I remember when I was a little girl the same thing happened to a dog we had, course now this was when Mama was living and Pa was home. Pa said he had rabies and had to be put down. I was just a little girl, as I said, but I remember the dog foaming at the mouth, and Mama wouldn't let me go out in the yard."

"Let me see your other hand," I requested. She looked at her hand that I had groomed, and kissed it.

"What about me? I did all the work." She handed me the other hand and smiled so big. "You ain't through yet."

"Well, I'll be through by the time you finish your dog story."

"Oh I almost forgot, I was tellin' about my dog wasn't I ? Where was I in the story?"

"The dog was lying on the end of the front porch foaming at the mouth."

"Oh yes, I was hoping my dog didn't have rabies...but by dinner time, he had killed both of my cats and was out in the back yard chasing my chickens."

"I'm almost scared to ask what happened next," I said as I kept right on working on her fingernails.

Chapter Three

"As Pa would say, 'when push came to shove', whatever that meant, I did what I had to. I thank the Lord for the rifle the old man gave me just before he died a while back. The dog was still running chickens and had caught one. I stepped to the back door," she pointed... "I took a bead with the rifle and shot the dog graveyard dead." She looked at her other hand that I had finished manicuring, rubbed her finger across her lips, and kissed it. "What about me?" I asked with a laugh.

"You ain't finished, yet!" She slid back enough to lay her foot in my lap, not paying any attention where her dress had gone. All I knew was that I had to get my eyes back in my head, and my mind on other things.

"You said an old man gave you the rifle just before he died." I began to examine her foot. She had beautiful small feet but they were in such bad shape. "Do you ever wear shoes?" I asked, as I began to massage her foot. She leaned back, bracing herself with her arms. "My, my, that feels good! You can do that all night."

"What about the shoes, and the old man?"

"I don't have any shoes to wear, and the old man died of gangrene in his leg. Could you do the other foot, some? It's kind of a long story, but not as long as my dog story. While you are trimming my toenails I will tell it to you...that is if you want to hear it."

"Oh yes, by all means, I want to hear about the dying man that gave you the rifle."

"Mother hadn't been dead long. It was a beautiful day and I thought I would wash some clothes and hang them on the line, since it was so pretty outside. I was minding my own business, chewing on a straw, with my arms in suds up to my elbows. Believe it or not, but I just felt somebody was staring a hole in my back. When I turned around I almost sucked the straw down my throat and peed in my panties." She paused and put her finger to her jaw as if in deep thought. "What is it? I asked.

"I don't know if I was wearing any underpants that day or not. I believe they were in wash."

"It doesn't make any difference, Mary. For Pete's sake! What about the old man staring a hole in you?"

"Well, as I was saying, there was the old codger standing not more than five or six feet from me. He was leaning on a homemade crutch and had a terrible odor. I think he knew he startled me.

'Don't be alarmed, Miss, I won't hurt you. Could you draw me a cool drink of water, and let me set in the shade of your front porch for a minute or so?'

'Oh no, I don't mind,' I said. I dropped the bucket in the well to get some fresh cool water, as he went hobbling toward the porch. I could tell he was having a hard time of it; his britches leg was split up to his knee, and black as a chunk of Empire coal. I carried him a dipper of cool water to drink, and he squared himself around leaning against a porch post, and began to drink.

'I know you are hungry, mister, let me run in the house and get you something to eat, you look mighty weak.' He took the dipper down, wiped his mouth on the back of his shirt sleeve, and started shaking his head. 'Save your food, young lady, I won't be here long enough to eat it. Take my rifle and possible bag. It is a present for you being so nice to me. You will find eighteen dollars and some change in my front pocket... that's for burying me when I die.' And that was the last word he ever spoke on this earth."

"Was he dead?" I asked.

"Don't take this as a short answer, Mr. Bill, he never drew another breath. I reckon so."

"My lord, what did you do then, Mary, since there wasn't anyone around the home place here to help you bury the old man... was there?"

"No, there wasn't, but I had 'im buried before he got stiff. I went around back and got Pa's makeshift wheelbarrow and drug him off the porch like a sack of taters. It was rough. I tell you I was slam out of breath time I rolled him down behind the field where you and I planted the two outlaws. Before you ask, I did get the money he had before I rolled him over in the hole." Mary turned around, leaned against me, and started looking at her toes.

"Well, what do you think, are you pleased?" I asked, as I put my arms around her waist and my chin on her shoulder.

"Have I been dreaming? What did you say your name was? Bill something or another, wasn't it?"

"It is Bill Allen from Atlanta. I just stopped by to be in your dream tonight."

"You hush now, I don't want to wake up if it is a dream." she said, taking hold of my hands and squeezing them tight to her body.

"Well, I know it's a dream," I whispered, letting my face touch her cheek, "because I'm dreaming, also." I had begun to doubt reality. Not more than four hours ago I was doubting if life was even worth living anymore. Now I'm sitting in the middle of the living room floor with my arms wrapped around a beautiful young woman who is just plain putty in my hands; and she would do anything for me I asked.

"Mary, can I ask you a big favor?" She quickly sprang to her knees, then turned around, and grabbing me around the neck. Her lips were near touching mine.

"I'll do anything you say, or give you anything you want, just say the word."

"Could I use your bath water, behind the wood stove, before it gets cold? I would at least like to wash my feet before I go to bed." I could tell her countenance fell, but quickly a grin came to her face. Then she smiled a big smile.

"I'll help you pull off your boots an' britches!"

"Just my boots and socks for now, Mary, please. I'll get the britches when I get over behind the stove." I held up each leg and off came each boot.

"Then, I'll just wash your back," she said, startin' over toward the wood stove with me.

"No, no Mary, that want be fair, I didn't get to wash your back." And before I could say pee-turkey she started taking off her dress. "Well we can even up this score. I didn't get enough of that sweet smellin' soap you brought."

"No! No, Mary!" I yelled. "Stop, stop! We must not look at each

17

other without any clothes on, you are a girl and I am a boy. And you are a grown girl now, and very pretty."

"I'm so sorry, Mr. Bill, I didn't know; I guess I haven't grown up yet in my mind."

"Well, you don't worry your pretty, little head over it. I will teach you if you want me to. I can also teach you how to read and write, if you would like."

"Oh yes, yes! I would like that very much, and the sooner the better."

"Okay, we'll start tomorrow. You go back over and sit down in front of the fire place and wait on me to take my bath. Oh, by the way, I been gonna ask you how old you are." She stopped and turned around. "I think I'm going on seventeen, I've kinda lost count though, since Mama died." I gave myself a good scrubbin' with a brush I found laying behind the stove; I near rubbed my hide off in a few places.

"I don't believe you are gonna get another washin' out of this water, black as it is."

"It's okay, I change it every Saturday anyway," Mary replied. I put my pants and my dry shirt back on and eased back over where Mary was waitin'.

"You acted upset because I was going to pull my dress off. You don't want to look at me without clothes?"

"Oh yes, I want to look at you in love, not lust."

"What is the difference?" Mary asked, movin' over close to me.

"What little I know, the dictionary definition of lust is intense or unrestrained sexual craving, or an overwhelming desire or craving. Lust has as its focus pleasing oneself, and it often leads to unwholesome actions to fulfill one's desires with no regard to the consequences.

You remember when I first rode up, what you asked me... 'You ain't gonna try nothing funny, are ya? Well, this is what your mama was talking about. When I want to undress you, it will be in love. I believe love is a sensation that magically generates when 'Mr. and Ms. Right' meet each other."

"Do you believe that God might have sent you by here for us to meet each other?"

"It's very possible, but I don't know the mind of God."

"Well I don't mind tellin' you, when you came I was at my rope's end, about to give up. You know that cow butter you smeared on the biscuits at supper?" I nodded, and she went on with her story. "Well, that's the last of the butter and cream, my cow died." Mary looked up at me with a very sad expression.

"Your cow died. . . just up and died?" I asked.

"Well, she didn't just up and die, it was more to it than I let on. You probably didn't notice it when you rode up this morning, but there is a big, tall pine tree out in the middle of our pasture, where the cows graze. It came up a lightning storm and lightning struck that tree and split it from top to bottom. Now, I didn't mind losin' the old tree, but my milk cow, this year's calf, last year's yearlin', and my bull, was standing under it and they all got killed, graveyard dead."

"What did you do?"

"It wasn't anything I could do but sit down and cry, but that wouldn't bring the cattle back. So, I did the next best thing I knew to do. There is a settlement of Black folks back down that way, so I tore off down to tell them they were welcome to the meat, before it all ruined. They brought me back with them, along with a couple of wagon,s and I was out of the cow business in one day."

"Now, I sure hate to hear that, Mary. Have you noticed how late it's gettin'."

"No, I haven't. I don't have a clock; well, I have one but it's broken and it wouldn't wind up. I just go to bed when I get sleepy."

"I'm gettin' a mite bit sleepy, how about you?" I asked Mary.

"Not really. I'm enjoying your company so much, it's better than sleep. Do you know how it is sleepin' in this house alone at night, not knowing what is going to break in on me? I'm so glad you are here. This will be the first night I haven't been scared in a long time."

"I'm so glad… I'm also glad I happened by, you have helped me as much as I've helped you."

"Does this mean I can sleep with you tonight? It sure would help me not to be so scared."

"I don't know, Mary, but if we do, you and I can't sleep close together."

"Oh, Bill, you can take my word, I won't even get close, just as long as we are in the same bed." It was dark over in the corner where the bed was settin'. I went over, pulled down to my long-handles, and eased under the quilt. I was facing the wall and not paying any attention to Mary when she came to bed. I could tell when she laid down and scooted under the cover.

I lay there thinking. I had a hard day and a long ride, and was almost asleep.

"Bill, Bill, are you asleep yet?"

"No, I'm not now, why?"

"Could you scratch my back? I can't get to where it's itchin'."

"Well, all right! Slide over this way. I laid my hand on her back between her shoulder blades. All I felt was skin, no clothes. I didn't say anything, thinking she might have pulled her night clothes around so I could scratch her back with ease. I began to scratch.

"It's further down, it itches a little further down." I let my hand slide down about half way and began to scratch her back, still only skin. "It's still a ways down, Bill, it still itches."

"But Mary, that's not your back, that is your butt, and did you pull off your dress?"

"Yes, I did. I didn't want to get it rumpled up. I'm gonna wear it to go to town with you tomorrow." I got her scratched and she slid back on her side of the bed. I rolled over thinkin' of the many nights I lay in a foxhole with bombs going off and mini balls whizzing over my head. I thought if I only had the warmth of a young woman laying beside me in a real bed, what I would do? Well, it's one thing for sure. I can get up in the morning with a clear conscience that this young girl won't have another little mouth to feed in nine months, after I'm gone.

When I woke up the next morning the sun shine was peepin' in, and Mary was all ready to go to town with me. Breakfast was ready and the table was set. "I was just fixin' to call you sleepy-head," she said as she walked over my way, drying her hands, "you ready for a cup of coffee?"

"Yes, I am, just as quick as I get my pants on and run to the outhouse." As soon as I came back and washed up, she and I sat down and began to eat. "Mary, that was the best night of rest I have had in years, what about you?" I noticed Mary shrugged her shoulders and twisted her mouth. "I just don't know, Bill, I wasn't scared, but I'm just plumb tuckered out this mornin'."

"My goodness, Mary, I was hopping things went well as they did for me." She started shaking her head as she poured us another cup of coffee. "I think I dreamed all night long about you and me. You seemed to keep gettin' yourself into bad situations that I had to keep gettin' you out of."

"I sure hate that, Mary, could you give me an example."

"I can give you a dozen...you were on top of this tall house and it was getting' dark as pitch and you couldn't get down."

"Why didn't I climb down like I got up on the house in the first place?"

"My dreams don't work like that. Another time you and I were out walking arm in arm having such a good time and I was waitin' for you to put your arms around me. Now guess what happened..this ferocious grizzly bear came chargin' out of the bushes, right for us. You told me to lie down and you would get rid of the bear."

"Now, I can very well see how that would interrupt your night's sleep."

"Well it did! He chased you for the longest."

"Why didn't you shoot the bear? You had a rifle."

"I thought about that right off, but I couldn't find that rifle high nor low. You see what I mean?"

"What happened next, when you couldn't find the rifle?"

"I woke up just wet with sweat, I rolled over and touched you to see if you were still here." I couldn't help but notice a loose board under the kitchen table while Mary was a tellin' her dream story.

"Excuse me a minute. I eased up and went over by the bed and brought back the big saddle bags with all the money in 'em. Mary watched as I eased down on my knees and lifted the loose board. I placed the saddle bag under the house and replaced the board. When I rose up I could tell Mary was confused, and had a thousand questions.

"There is money, lots of money in those bags. If anything ever happens to me, it is yours. Never tell anyone."

Chapter Four

Let's go to town, are you ready?" I felt so bad to see a grown woman walk out that front door going to town without any shoes on, it hurt me. Maybe God did send me by here, if only to buy her some shoes for this winter coming on.

The town of Evart sits right on the Alabama and Mississippi border line, and I was hoping they had a shoe store, at least. As she and I rode into town it was apparent they were having some type of shindig going on. There were banners and decoration in store windows and along the street.

Mary and I headed straight for the clothing store. She didn't know it yet, but I was going to dress her up in style. Mary was very petite and very easy to buy for; most everything fit her. When I got through with her she was something else, fit to kill you might say... all new boots, belt, and britches, and she had what it took to fill out a pair of denim jeans. Didn't anyone have to tell her how to strut her stuff. She was in hog heaven. We even went to a café to eat dinner.

We found out it was Election Day. The town was voting on a Mayor and havin' a big barn dance this evening in the park. Well, neither of us could dance, but she and I didn't see anything wrong watching the others. She and I were having a ball eating and drinking the free food and drink. After Mary and I finished our shopping, we managed to tie our clothes and food stuff behind our saddle, in an orderly fashion, and moseyed on over to the dance that was just getting started.

I wasn't ashamed to walk with Mary now; she was wearing her new outfit and getting a few stares from the onlookers, especially the men. I guess we had been there the better part of an hour watchin' the excitement. All of a sudden these two young men came ridin' up. The younger one shot up in the air several times and slid out of the saddle. I just reckoned they wanted to be noticed more than anything, and to let everybody know they had arrived. When they dismounted, it was plain to see they were well liquored up. The duet stood for a minute looking all around.

Soon the younger of the two came walking straight toward us, like a purple martin to a gourd.

"Let's us dance a little jig, baby!" he said to Mary, grabbin' her by the arm.

"I don't dance! she scolded, and moved closer to me. I thought that was the last of 'em, and if I would have used any judgment at all... Mary and I should have left the dance and started back to her house, right then. I watched him as he milled around the crowd sluggin' down his corn liquor, getting drunker and drunker by the minute. I guess when he finished up his bottle he got enough nerve to stagger back over.

"Girl, I guess you don't know who I am, but I know who you are. You are old man Walter Brook's daughter. I heard he got shot for desertion at the battle of Hill Creek."

"I do know who you are, too...Bo Irwin... now you go on and leave me alone." He took Mary by the arm again and started pulling her out where the dance was. She snatched loose again, and ran back to me.

"Sir, the young lady has told you twice she don't dance, now you better go on and leave her alone."

"She ain't a lady. She lives by herself and needs a good taking care of."

"She is my girl, an' I'll do the takin' care of her. I highly suggest you leave her alone."

"I don't believe you know who I am, stranger." Then he grabbed for Mary again. I quickly stepped between the two, and gave him a shove. Well, he got tangled up in his spurs, then tripped and fell down. I could tell it embarrassed him, but that was no excuse for dying. "Somebody needs to teach you a lesson, stranger," he said as he drew his pistol. Oh well, that was the last mistake he made on God's green earth. I drew and shot him in the chest, hoping his body would stop the bullet so it could not hit anyone on the other side of him.

The young man, no older than I, stopped the bullet all right, but didn't stop his brother. "Do you know who you just shot?" a voice yelled out. "That was my brother, let me get my rifle." I watched as he ran to his horse and got his rifle, and here he came running back on the dance floor. I cocked my Colt and waited as he injected a round in the chamber, and then I cut him down. It was a fair fight, but one could hear whispers through the crowd, "Does the stranger know who he just killed?" I holstered my pistol and waited. If I had known then what I know now, I would have gotten on my horse and been long gone.

"Someone get the sheriff!" This was repeated several times among the crowd. And speaking of the devil, here he came: a red faced, overweight individual, smoking a cigar and cursing every breath. When he saw that I had killed the bank president's two sons, that's all it took. He closed his mind to the few standing around that were telling him it was a fair fight. and it was self defense.

The sheriff began to snatch me around like I was a red-headed step child, cursin' every breath.

"Boy, you are a dead man walking. When Mr. Irwin comes in from Birmingham tomorrow, he will have you hung for killin' his two boys. What a blow this will be; he just buried his wife about a month ago."

"I deserve a fair trial, Sheriff," I pleaded, just as two of his deputies nearly broke my arms hauling me off to jail.

"You're gonna get a fair trial, just before we hang you tomorrow ,boy." I looked all around for Mary and didn't see her anywhere. I remembered what a man told my pa one time, 'Mr. Allen I will stick with you through thick and thin, but when it gets too thick I'm gonna thin out'.

The turnkey at the jail seemed to be a decent sort. After the dust and smoke settled and every one went home, he was sitting out front with his boots propped up on a desk, dozin' in and out. "What chance you think I have tomorrow. old timer?" I ask the gentleman out front.

"Are you speaking to me, young fellow?" He arose and walked back to the cell where I was, looking at me through the bars.

I asked again, "What chance do you think I have tomorrow at my trial? It was self defense you know."

"It doesn't matter, son you don't have the chance, as a snow ball in hell not melting."

I went back to my bunk, lay down, and began to think. Well, I guess I will never see Mary again, unless she comes to my hanging. I know I fell in love with that little girl, and I believe she did me. Why did we have to come to town, anyway? To make matters even worse, a lightning storm came up, and you never heard the like. Lightning was striking all around the jail. I thought one time I'd about as soon be killed by lightning rather than getting hung. I even thought about that dream Mary was telling me about; how I was always getting myself in a predicament and she was trying to get me out. Well, this time I think had bitten off more than I could chew.

There was no going to sleep with the storm going on and me thinking about tomorrow. I guessed it was about midnight and the storm hadn't let up, but had gotten worse, if you ask me. It was then I felt something hit my leg. I didn't pay any attention, because I thought the roof was gonna fall in on me at any time. Then I heard something hit the wall close to my head and bounce on the floor. It was dark, except for the light of a coal-oil lantern hanging just outside my cell. I reached down and searched around with my hand, and found a small rock. As I picked it up from the floor, here came another one that hit me. By this time I discovered they were coming through the only window in the cell. For a minute I thought the wind was blowing the rocks through the window. I leaned up and trained my eyes on the window, which faced a back alley. This is when I heard a strange sound - a spewing sound - as if some one was trying to get my attention.

I jumped up suddenly and ran to the shoulder high window . Lo and behold, there was Mary, threading a rope through the iron bars.

"Tie it on to the bars tight!" she whispered as she disappeared into the dark. By then I had put two and two together. I quickly tied a double blood knot to three of the iron bars in the window, and stepped back, waiting for the window to go flying through the air. I knew, just by looking that the jail was cheaply built, made of poorly laid bricks and stucco.

Not only did the window disappear from my vision, but the whole back wall was now lying out in the back alley. What really surprised me was that it hardly made any noise. I doubt if the old man in the front heard it over the thunder and lightning.

Mary had put a horse-collar on my horse and tied the rope to it. (She said later she didn't want to hurt my horse.) I quickly disposed of the rope and horse-collar, and she and I headed west. We didn't say much until we knew we were safely out of town. By this time we were soaking wet and shivering cold. We knew we needed to get dry and warm. We had two things going for us; it had almost quit raining and was just about daylight.

"Look, Mary, there is an old barn sitting out in a field. It looks as if the house is burned down." We turned our horses and headed to the barn, hoping to build a fire and get warm and dry, before we caught our death. She and I rode under a shed attached to what was left of the old barn. There we tied our horses. I didn't have to do much to build a fire; someone in the past had carefully placed a circle of rocks so the fire could be contained. I even noticed some fire wood was left behind. With a hand full of old dry hay, a match, and a prayer ,the fire was going.

I pulled Mary to me, with my arms tight around her waist. At first she didn't know what was going on.

"I can't believe you did what you did last night. Why did you risk your life for me?"

"You don't remember what you said to Bo Irwin, just before you shot him?" I shook my head and pulled her even closer.

"You told him I was your girl. If I'm your girl, then you're my man," she said, looking up into my eyes. For the first time I let my lips touch her lips, as she put her arms around my neck.

"You kissed me! You like me some, don't you, Bill?" Big tears came to Mary's eyes.

"No, I don't like you, I love you, and I love you with all my heart! But we have lots to talk about." She and I put on some clothes that were rolled up behind the saddle, and luckily had not gotten wet. We set our boots by the fire to get dry then she and I spread one of our blankets on some dry hay, against the wall of the old barn. I took Mary in my arms; we lay down and covered ourselves with the other blanket. We got 'as snug as a bug in a rug', as they say.

"Mary, I know you went over to your house after they put me in jail, did you think to get the saddle bag from under the house?"

"Yes, I did, and I brought some dishes and the coffee pot. Do you want me to make us some coffee? It sure would go good about now."

"That would be very nice of you. One other question, what about the hogs and chickens you left behind? You may never see them again."

"Oh, I know, I opened the gate and let them out. They will fend

26

for themselves all right. Darling, if I never see that place again it will never matter, as long as I have you."

"Do you know what you just called me?"

"Oh, Mr. Bill, I'm so sorry, I never want to do or say anything to offend you in any way. I will never call you Darling, again." I grabbed her and pulled her face very close to mine, as if I was mad. I think, in a way, I scared her.

"You just better call me Darling, again or I will be mad." I knew from that minute on I had the lovingest little lady a man could ever hope for. She and I did some more loving, finished the pot of coffee, and packed it up along with the blankets. Mary also thought to bring the extra pistol we took from the outlaws that we had buried behind the forty acre field. I made sure it was loaded and in working order, and we saddled up to ride.

Now the way I saw it, the more space she and I had between us and the town of Evart the better off we were. Of course, after I broke out of jail it rained the rest of the night, so tracking us would be impossible; besides, the sheriff had no idea which direction we went. To my way of thinking, he probably would go over to Mary's house to look for me. And I would think after he sobered up and talked with some of the town's people, he might get highly discouraged trying to get up a posse. From what scuttlebutt Mary had heard around town, the Allen boys were bullies and no one liked them, and I might have done the town of Evart a favour.

"You know, Mr. Bill, my feet have swelled or these new boots are getting littler," Mary said, propping her leg up in the saddle.

"Maybe all that kissing made your feet grow."

"Well if that's the case, I'll just wear tight boots, I ain't gonna give up my kissing, since I just got it started." I couldn't help but laugh, a little dumb and a little smart, I thought. How I love that girl! I've known her only a few days, and if I run across a preacher, I'm going to ask Mary to marry me.

Now, I didn't know where we were going. I had no time limit or no certain day to be anywhere. Actually I was enjoying myself, riding along with Mary, talking and stopping now and then to eat and sleep. As Mary and I crossed the state of Mississippi we would ask directions how to go out west, and where we could cross the muddy Mississippi.

It was the second or third day of riding, still heading west according to the compass I carried in my pocket. Mary's boots had loosened up and we were in good shape. As we rounded a bend in the rather good road, we saw a bunch of folks standing up ahead.

"I guess someone is broke down," Mary said, stretching her neck to look.

"Well, we'll soon find out," I answered. As Mary and I approached the goings-on up ahead, I noticed the covered wagon was a Conestoga, a rather large wagon. It was behind a buck-board.

"Howdy-do, can I help you folks in some way?" I asked, as I pulled my horse up to a stop. "No, just stopped to blow for a spell," the older man standing next to the buck-board., said. The couple standing by the back of the covered wagon never did say anything. Looking out of the back of the covered wagon was a young boy and girl, and an older girl, who looked to be thirteen or fourteen years-old, stood alone beside the big wagon, near the water barrel. Mary rode on over to where the young girl was standing and stopped her horse. She began talking to the girl.

Chapter Five

"You sure have pretty, long hair," Mary said to the young girl standing alone.

"Would you like to have a drink of water?" she asked Mary.

"I don't mind if I do," said Mary, who turned side ways and slid out of the saddle. She walked over to the young lady with the long hair, who in turn handed her a dipper full of water. Mary drank the water down, thanked the young lady, and hugged her neck. I was ready to go, but Mary stood for a second and caught my gaze. Then she mounted her horse.

"Well, if you folks don't need no help, we're gonna mosey on," I said, starting down the road minding my on business. I noticed Mary lagged behind, but soon caught up.

"Did you notice anything wrong with them folks back there?"

"Can't say that I did. In what way are you speaking?"

"Well, the old man standing by the buck-board and the young man on the horse holding a shotgun in his lap, they just didn't look like the others."

"You are right about them not looking alike, but as far as the shotgun, I didn't see any scabbard on his horse to put it in. Then again, he didn't know who we were, riding up on them."

"But Bill, darling, it's what the young girl said to me after I handed her the dipper back."

"Do remember what she said?"

"Yes! She said, 'Help us,' as if the old man and the boy on the horse was threatening them in some way."

"Now that you mentioned it, the man and woman did look frightened, and never said a word, did they?" I said, looking back.

"You think maybe you and I ought to go back and check on 'em? They may be in danger."

"Well, we can, but if they are road-agents they are going to put up a fight, and you know what that means?"

"Yes, I do. Someone is gonna get shot, if I know you."

"What do you mean, if you know me? I don't like killing."

"No, Bill, what I meant was, you sure know how to use your pistol. I saw you draw on Bo Irwin."

"Well, it ain't no telling how many Yankees I maimed or killed in some way while I was in the war. And now that I'm out of the service, I've already killed four men."

"Are you saying you don't want to get mixed up in their problem?"

"No, I'm not saying that at all." I stopped right in the middle of the road. "You want to go back and help that young girl, don't you?"

"Yes, but I don't want you to get hurt either."

"We'll just have to take our chances, let's go back." She and I whipped our horses around about the same time and headed back. When we rounded the curve there they sat, less one buck-board and one man on a horse. When we came closer, the young girl recognized Mary and came running toward us.

"You've come back to help us, haven't you?" We dismounted, and Mary started talking to the young girl. I made my way over to the man and woman to see what had happened. She was still crying.

"What happened?" I asked, as if I didn't know.

"The old man and boy robbed us at gunpoint, and took everything we had, even the few dollars we saved up to go west."

"They said they would kill us if we spoke out while you and your wife were here," the woman said, still crying.

"Well, don't worry, ma'am, I'll get all your stuff back...And the young lady over there who was talking to your daughter is my girl friend, but soon as we find a preacher we are going to get married."

"Young fellow, my name is Terry Mason and my wife is Dorothy. We can do some bartering if you are game. I'm an ordained Minister. Just let me know when you are ready to get hitched, and the wife and I will do the rest."

"Oh well, I haven't asked my girl friend yet, but we do need to talk about the two men that robbed you. I need to catch them before it gets dark and too far away."

"First of all, Mister..." he started to say, as I butted in.

"My name is Bill Allen and my girlfriend is Mary Brooks, and you were saying?"

"Well, Bill Allen, the wife and I don't believe in violence, but they took everything we had to live on. We were carrying sacks of dry beans, meal, coffee, and sugar, not to mention the cans of syrup and lard. We also had lots of canned fruit and smoked hams. Actually, they were loaded and near ready to go when you all came by a while ago," said the preacher man.

"We would have not come back at all if it hadn't been for your daughter talking to Mary. She said, 'Help us'. Now do you folks need some help, or do you want to sit right here and let your children starve to death?"

"What do you think will happen when you approach the ol' man and young lad that have all of our food in their wagon?" the preacher asked, hoping I could talk them out of the food they had just stolen.

"Just what would you do, Reverend Mason, if you were an out law, and all you ever did was rob and steal? Let me answer that question for you...when I catch up to the old man and his boy, and he gets a good look at me, he'll know who I am and he'll start shooting. Now I ask you, what do you want me to do - let him fill me full of holes - and bring your wagon load of food back?" He and his wife looked at each other, not knowing what to say.

"We have always believed in not using violence, and the Lord will fight our battles."

"Do you both agree to that decision? If you do, then my girl friend and I will head on west." I started back to my horse.

"Are you ready to go, sweetheart? The Lord is coming by after a while to give this family a hand."

"Now, Bill Allen, you know better than that!" she scolded while walking toward me leading her horse. As it was, she walked right on past me and stopped right in front of Rev. and Mrs. Mason.

"I heard what you said to Bill; you two don't believe in violence! Well, we don't either, but who do you think sent us back to help you folks...the tooth fairy?" They both looked at each other again.

"Do you think we may need to reconsider, Grace?" Rev. Mason asked his wife. "Since you said Bill doesn't believe in violence, what might his plans be, do you think?"

"Let me answer a question, with a question. Do you folks have a shovel, or did the ol' man take that, also?" Mary asked. Rev. and Mrs. Mason looked dumbfounded, then answered the question.

"Yes, we have a brand new shovel."

"Good! Let's go get the wagon, Bill, darling." Mary and I didn't say another word, but mounted up and rode off, leaving the family standing with open mouths. The buck-board was easy to track; it was heavy and the ground was still damp.

"Now, Mary, here is our plan; when we get in sight of the buck-board let's turn off and go through the woods around them, and meet them head on."

"That is a good idea! I was thinking that idea to myself all the time."

"Were you thinking you might have to use that rifle you are carrying?"

"No, that thought never crossed my mind," Mary answered.

"Well, pull it out of your scabbard and make sure it is loaded, and watch that boy on the horse like a hawk." I went ahead and removed the thong off the hammer of my trusty Colt.

"There they are, Bill." Without further ado Mary and I turned off the main road and kicked our horses to get around the wagon. We were spaced out, sitting right in the middle of the road, when the old man, and the boy on the horse, came around the curve.

"What do y'all want?" the old man asked, as he glanced over at the boy with a surprised look.

"Oh, we just stopped to blow for a spell." I could tell he had heard this line before, as he grabbed for his pistol...that was the second mistake he had made today. As I fired, I heard another shot and watched as the boy on the horse went tumbling to the ground. The old man stood up, dropped his pistol, and fell back in the wagon.

"Help me load the boy up, Dear," I had already drug him over behind the wagon before Mary dismounted and slowly eased over my way.

"Is he dead?" she asked.

"Dead as a door nail."

"Well, I don't know if I meant to kill him."

"Then why did you shoot 'im?" I asked, throwing his carcass in the back of the buck-board. "You bring the horses and I'll drive the wagon." I turned the rig around, and facing the evening sun I started back. The whole kit and caboodle were standing in the middle of the road waiting when we drove up.

"We'll need that shovel now, Reverend Mason,." Mary said in a sad voice

"Let me help you, Bill. At least I can help bury them and say a few words over their bodies." The preacher eased up in the wagon with me and shook his head. He and I drove down the road a ways to bury the men.

Before I rolled him over in the hole, I went through the old man's pockets and gave the preacher back the money they had robbed from him I also kept his gun rigging, and the shot gun and shells the younger fellow kept waving around. We were back at the covered wagon in time to get unloaded and help the women folk to fix us supper.

During supper we sat around and talked, and planned out a strategy for crossing the State of Mississippi until we reached Vicksburg, where we would cross the river. Rev. Mason explained how his family was to meet others in Vicksburg who were heading west also. I warned him of the danger of going alone in times like these. Today was no exception. There would be outlaws, thugs, carpet-baggers, road-agents and swindlers every step of the way.

"Live by the gun, die by the gun," the reverend stated as we finished up our supper.

"Yes, and Sam Colt said: 'God made man, and I made them equal'. I took out my pistol and spun the cylinder, this is all the bad men respect, they don't know who God is."

"Well, I'm going out west to teach them, and there will be no need for guns," he said.

"That is a good dream, Reverend Mason, and I'm all for it, I'm tired of killing men...But if you don't mind, I'll keep wearing my Colt until this all comes to pass.

"We should be in Vicksburg by Thursday, if our good pace holds out and it don't rain," said the preacher."

"I know what you mean, sir. It ain't too bad on the horses, but the swift water wants to wash the wagons down stream. And we best not cross any rivers or streams that are raging with high water from the rain." I could tell the preacher had something on his mind and he just couldn't seem to get it out.

"Bill, I need to talk to you about something very important," the preacher waited until the ladies started clearing the dishes after supper. "You know, after you gave me the money back the old man took from me." I nodded that I remembered this is what I had done.

"Well, it was nearly a hundred dollars too much, after I counted it." He tried to hand a wad of bills back to me. I shook my head in disgust, "Brother, you wouldn't know a blessing from God if it hit you right in the face." I could tell I had upset the preacher by my remark. But he listened, although his face turned red.

"I'll tell you what you can do. Our animals need grain...so the next feed store we come across, use that money to treat the horses. And thank God for a buck-board to haul the extra load." The preacher still didn't say anything but seem to regain his composure.

"You know, Bill, the Lord does work in mysterious ways," he said as he put the money back in his pocket.

I was wondering why Reverend Mason hadn't mentioned anything else about Mary and me getting married in the last day or two. But Mary found out from Susie, the thirteen year old girl with the beautiful long hair. She let it be know she had heard her mother and father talking about how Mary was sinning before God.

Mary said, " Susie took the Bible and showed it to me. You know I can't read, but I memorized what it said in the Bible. She used that big word, Deuteronomy 22:5: 'The woman shall not wear that which pertaineth unto a man, for all that do so are abomination unto the Lord thy God.'"

"Let me get this straight in my mind now, Mary... Reverend Mason will not marry us because you are wearing denim jeans?"

"That's right, I didn't want to say anything to you about it because you bought these britches for me, and I'm proud to have something to wear besides that one worn-out dress."

"Well if that don't beat it all, that is what I thought, the reverend's whole religious beliefs is around do's and don'ts."

"You know, Bill, darling, a piece of paper that says we're married is not going to make our love making any sweeter."

"No, I reckon not, but it sure would keep us from busting hell wide open."

"Let's just change the subject. I'm looking forward to getting to Vicksburg, aren't you?" Mary asked with enthusiasm.

"It's like this. Mary I can take 'em, or pass 'em by; my druthers is setting on a creek bank fishing."

"Do you want me along with you?"

"Might as well."

To say that the city of Vicksburg was a major player in the

American Civil War is an understatement. In fact, the southern city was nicknamed, "The Key to the South." Because of its location atop a high bluff overlooking the muddy Mississippi River, Vicksburg was nearly invincible to Union troops, and it was a lifeline to the Confederacy because it allowed the South to control one of the most vital supply and trade water routes for much of the war.

President Abraham Lincoln knew gaining control of this artery would restore trade to the north and cut off major supply lines to the Confederacy. With that in mind, the Vicksburg battle known as "The Siege of Vicksburg" began. Lasting 47 days, the siege became the turning point in the Civil War.

Chapter Six

When we finally made it to Vicksburg, we met with three of the families that had arrived earlier. They were patiently waiting for Reverend Mason and the other wagons to show up at anytime. They had camped on the east end of town, and were no trouble to find.

After several hours, Mary and I had met everyone and decided to walk into town to see the sights. Nothing would do Susie but to tag along. It seemed that Mary, who was not much older than she, had made quite an impression on young Susie's life. Rev. and Mrs. Mason were some what hesitant at first to let her go, with Mary still wearing britches. But Mary, now knowing Rev. Mason's feelings, was gonna wear her britches if it hair-lipped everyone in the City of Vicksburg.

I could tell that Vicksburg had made a great transition, and was coming back stronger than before the War Between the States. Of course, this encouraged the scum-bums, the low life bootleggers, and prostitutes to swarm the red-light district of Vicksburg like flies on a dead cow. I could also tell, if you had money, you could get anything you wanted in this town. I could see why Rev. and Mrs. Mason nearly protested the thirteen year old daughter going with us.

The three of us were going in and out of shops and stores looking. I even bought me, and Mary, a two shot Derringer apiece. Susie and Mary thought it was neat for us to go into a café, sit down, and be waited on. After our lunch, we began to sight see and just have fun, going our own way, doing our own thing. The problem with that scenario was: we took our eyes off Susie.

"Have you seen Susie?" Mary asked.

"No, I thought she was with you," I answered.

"Well, I thought she was followin' you around. I know one thing, we'd better find her. From the looks of this crowd ,I don't feel safe myself." Mary and I searched, and even back-tracked the way we came, and still no sight of Susie.

"You don't think maybe she thought we went off and left her, do you?" I asked. I was grasping for straws.

"Are you saying she couldn't find us, and just maybe she started on back to the wagon?" Mary asked, while standing on tiptoe, stretching her neck and lookin' all about.

"I don't know, but I don't know where else to look, either," I said.

"It is getting late. and her daddy will be looking for us, before much longer," Mary said, taking me by the arm.

"We might as well hot foot it back to the wagon and, see if Susie might have come back... time's a wasting."

"If she ain't at the wagon, what are we going to tell her folks?" Mary asked, catching my gaze.

"It ain't nothing we can do, but tell them the truth," I said. Mary's eyes got really big, as if she had seen a ghost.

"What is it!?" I said.

"What I'm thinkin', I shouldn't have thought it!" Mary shook her head.

"What are you thinkin'?" I quickly asked, already knowing the answer.

"She has been kidnapped, right under our noses."

"I'm afraid you are right, Mary."

"Well what are we going to do if it's true?"

"First of all, let's don't start jumping to conclusions; we need to make sure she is gone, before we start worryin'."

When Mary and I got back to the wagon train, the other family, from down in Florida, had arrived. These were the ones that the others had been waitin' on. I think these were some church friends that also had the notion of joining the wagon train headed out west. There was such a celebration going on that the folks hardly noticed we had come back from town. Both Mary and I began to scan the crowd...but no Susie.

"What are we to do?" Mary asked. I moved through the bystanders until I reached Rev. and Mrs. Mason.

"Sir, me and Mary need to talk to you and your wife; it's very important!" All of a sudden a strange feeling came over me; it was as if the Masons already knew what had happened to their daughter.

"Susie didn't come back with you, did she?" Rev. Mason asked. Now you could have knocked me over with a chicken feather.

"How did you know, Sir?" I quickly asked.

"Oh, we just knew, we been waiting on that rebellious Jezebel spirit to raise its ugly head in Susie, for some time." That was all mumbo-jumbo to me; it went straight over my head. Mary just stood there like a day-old calf looking at a forty acre field of red clover.

"Look, Reverend Mason, you are talkin' to a young lady that can't even read or write her own name, and me... a red neck from Georgia. What's all this religious rhetoric?" Both his and his wife's face turned red as a turkey snout as they looked at each other.

"Susie is not our own biological child," said the preacher sadly.

"Good Lord, man! You act iffen you're glad Susie is gone."

"You two wouldn't understand what we have gone through with that rebellious child, ever since the wife and I adopted her, when she was a baby."

"I think you are the very ones that don't understand...Susie went off with us, and we didn't bring her back to where we took her off from."

"Look, Bill and Mary, don't blame yourself. This was going to happen sooner or later, anyway."

"Now you wait just one damn second, we don't believe 'what will be, will be', for one cotton picking minute."

"Are you saying it was bred into Susie to run away? For Pete's sake, man, she is only thirteen. Me and Mary thinks she has been kidnapped by the underworld criminals here in Vicksburg."

Mr. Mason took his wife's hand and turned to walk away. "We'll be praying about the situation, that's all we can do, now." And they left me and Mary standin' there like two totem-poles.

"Well, if that don't beat all!" Mary said, looking at me and twisting her mouth.

"Well, I'm gonna find that girl if it's the last thing I ever do. If she has been kidnapped, then someone in Vicksburg Mississippi knows where she is."

"You are not going to let me go with you?" Mary asked.

"No, my dear, I will be workin' under cover, but you can help me load the little Derringers I bought for us."

"You are not going to carry your side arm?"

"Oh no! It will stand out like a King James Bible on a hardwood bar. Don't you worry now, I'll be back soon."

I saddled my horse, Buddy, and rode off to where we first missed Susie. I tied Buddy in a park type place where there was ample grass. The crowd had thinned out as I began to pound the pavement. It was getting near sundown, and the street lights were slowly being lit. It was once said that the snakes crawl at night, the appearance of the night crowd had changed from bad to worse. The street walkers and pimps were making their way on the scene like maggot larva being hatched on a dead carcass.

I didn't think it was such a good idea to bring my horse for someone to steal. Oh well ,I thought, I'd try to keep an eye on Buddy the best I could. I was like a house fly sitting on a churn full of cream; I didn't quite know where to start first. I kept watching a colored boy, about twenty years of age, walkin' up and down the street, making conversation with the girls of the night.

I walked across the street and started looking all around, as if I was planning to buy the place. The young black man caught my gaze and here he came, doing a little shuffle with his feet as he approached me. Before he had time to say anything, I spoke out.

"Pardon me, Sir, I'm from Atlanta, Georgia, headin' west and looking for a good time tonight." The black boy sort of pulled his neck down in his shoulders and sheepishly looked all around.

"I guess you talkin' to me...well, white boy, you have brung yore self to the right end of Vicksburg." He looked all around again. "Man, just any of my girls can show you a good time tonight."

"These girls are old enough to be my mama." I took a rather large bill out of my pocket and waved it under is nose. "I'm looking for someone, young man." I paused and looked all around. "You know, who could be my little sister, if you get what I'm saying." The black boy reached for the money, but I said, "You ain't told me nothing yet man."

"Okay, okay, you need to go to Sadie's, on the hill," he said, and he reached for the bill again.

"Not so fast, my man, I told you I was new in town, and I don't know where 'Sadie's on the hill' is any more than I know where to find Buffalo Bill!"

"Come on I'll show you." He and I hurried to the end of the block, and he pointed to a Victorian style house that could very well have been the Governor's Mansion. I gave the boy the bill and started up a hill, to the house where a red lantern hung on the front porch. I can say one thing, I wasn't by my self. There were men, young and old, coming and goin' in and out. I stopped at the big front door, brushed my feet on the welcome mat, and turned the big brass door knob. As I stepped inside, where the devils hang out, I knew this was a wicked place.

"Can I help you, young man? My, my, you are so handsome!" A soft voice came from an older but beautiful woman sitting on a love seat beside the door. She was not wearing much more than a smile on her face. "Why yes, you can...and can I say your perfume is heavenly? The aroma is almost breath takin'!" I exclaimed, after taking a deep breath.

"Oh my, I think I'll keep you out here with me." I walked over to where she was. She quickly moved around where I could sit down. I leaned over, and my lips rubbed her cherry red lips.

"You must be Sadie; I've been looking for you all over the world." She kissed me on my lips and gently shoved me away, then straightened up. My, my, how you carry on! Where were you when I was nineteen? You know what I'm gonna do for you to night, Sonny Boy? You can have a free one."

"Oh really?" I questioned.

"That's right, young man. Just pick your lady for the evening."

"Could you give me someone that has been working here for a long time?" I requested, as I stood up.

"That would be Debbie, she knows how to show a young man a wonderful night." Sadie motioned for Debby sitting across the room; she smiled from ear to ear, jumpin' up and runnin' over. "Now Honey Child, you take my boy in the back and give him anything he wants; and it's on the house." I leaned over again and gave Sadie a kiss. Debbie took my hand and led me down a hall to a very plush back room. It was like out of a book I had once seen, silk pillows and miles of lace

"Sadie tells me you have been working for her a long time."

"Oh yes, it seems like forever. Sadie is just like a mother to me. And she said I am to give you anything you want."

"Well, I asked Sadie to give me a lady who knows all about Vicksburg; one who has seen and heard what's going on in the underworld..." Debbie stopped pulling off her clothes and sat down on the side of the big soft bed.

"You are not going to get me in trouble, are you?"

"Oh, no, I'm just passing through," I explained. And I proceeded to tell Debbie my whole story...from the war to the Atlanta fire, to my folks dying, and how I met my girlfriend.

"It was late yesterday evening - myself, Mary, and the girl I speak of, was going in and out shops and stores on Main Street. I looked around and discovered that Susie had gone missing, nowhere to be found. Me and Mary went out looking and looking, but we never found her."

"How old did you say Susie was? And you think she has been kidnapped and sold into prostitution?"

"Yes, I do. she is only thirteen, and still a virgin, according to Mary - she's my girlfriend."

"I can say one thing; she won't be working in or around any well known parlor houses that I know of. I know I haven't been much help, but you need to talk to Ray Fleming. He works part time for Sadie and does her dirty work, if some needs to be done. Just don't ask me what he does. I may have to tell you a few lies." We both had a belly laugh.

"Could I ask you where I might find him?"

"What I can do is start screaming. Then he would come busting through that door."

"Please don't do that! Just tell me where to find him."

"When you leave this room. go straight down the hall and out the back door. He will probably be settin' on the back porch chewing tobacco and spittin' it out in the yard."

"I know this is a free one., but can I give you a tip?"

"You can if you want to. Just don't tell Sadie or the others." I reached in my pocket an' drug out a wad of bills that would have choked a small billy goat. I peeled a fifty off the top and handed it to Debby.

"Oh my, my, oh my." She said jumping up grabbing me around the neck and squeezing me so tight my neck popped.

I eased on out of the room and made my way on down the hall, trying not to disturb anyone's pleasure. And sure enough, there sat Ray Fleming, chewing and spitting.

"Are you Ray Fleming?" I asked, propping up on a porch post.

"That's me, and who might you be?"

"My name is Bill Allen from Atlanta, Georgia, and I'm heading west." I went ahead and unloaded all my troubles on the man. I don't think I left a stone unturned.

"Come on around and set down I will tell you what I know. First of all, you will be dealing with a mean bunch of bastards from New Orleans. They'd just as soon kill you as look at you. Now, Bill, I know what they do, but I don't know who's doing the dirty work."

"Maybe you could point me in the right direction, and get me started."

He spit a stream of tobacco juice out in the yard, which would have knocked a small dog down, and handed me his plug.

I shook my head no. "I think I'll pass, but thanks anyway."

Chapter Seven

Ray continued with his story, "As I was saying, you will be dealing with a mean bunch of cut throats that don't have the morals of an alley cat. These sons of a bitch will kidnap a thirteen-year old girl and sell her to a rich rice or sugarcane tycoon in New Orleans. They'll have sex with her, which butchers her virginity. Many times the girls bleed to death, while the men get their pleasure watching them." The more I heard, the more my blood boiled.

"You are saying these men kidnap these young girls and sell their bodies to rich men in New Orleans?"

"Not only New Orleans, but Chicago and New York. . .why that young thirteen-year old girl you speak of will sell for over a thousand dollars, if these scum bags can get her to the right man. Let me ask you something, Bill, where were you when the young girl came up missing?"

"Well, this we are not sure of. The three of us somehow got split up after about five minutes, or a little longer."

"If these men, or it could be a woman, is still working the same way, five minutes is plenty of time. Did you and your girl friend walk past anybody that wanted to take your picture for free? Or did you come past any one sitting in a nook wanting to tell your fortune for free?"

"Why, yes, we did." It was like a light came on in my head.

"Then this is where they nabbed the girl. They gag her where she can't scream, and out the back door they drag her to a covered wagon. Then they take her to a holding house where they lodge the girls. A boat runs each week from New Orleans and collects the girls these crooks have kidnapped."

"I believe what you are saying, Mr. Ray, tell me more."

"Look, Bill! I haven't been keeping up with this bunch of hoodlums, I got problems of my own. Iit ain't a week passes I don't have to beat someone within an inch of their life, or kill them. Have you ever killed a human being, I mean graveyard dead?" I could tell just talkin' about this got Mr. Ray's dander up.

"Yes sir, Mr. Ray, I have killed five men already."

"Well, I'm sure they needed it, and your killin' ain't stopped. Before you get the young girl back, you will have to kill a bunch of these sons of a bitch. and I hope you stack 'em up like cord wood in the winter time."

"Mr. Ray, you have given me a place to start, and I sure do thank you. I already have a plan to find the girl."

"More power to you, young man, one other thing I might add ,they may be keeping the girls on a river boat tied up down below the hill."

I thanked Mr. Ray Fleming and ran back down town, hoping someone hadn't swiped my horse.

"Thank the Lord," I murmured to myself. There Buddy stood, right where I left him, still nibbling on grass. What really got my goat, when I arrived at the camp the preacher or his wife didn't say one word to me about Susie! I guess they saw I didn't bring her back with me, and out of sight, out of mind.

Mary greeted me just a fumin', "I don't know about this bunch of religious fanatics you and I are hanging out with. I found out while you were gone that three of the men driving the wagons are preachers like Rev. Mason, and they look at me like I'm trash."

"All I can say is just don't worry your pretty lil' ol" head over it; when I was a small boy, Mama would say these folks would gag at a gnat but swallow a camel." While I was gone, and before it got dark Mary had gone to the trouble to pile some pine straw under the buck-board ,and spread our blanket for our bed.

"At least if it rains tonight, we won't get soaked," she said as she and I crawled under the wagon. "It will keep the night dew off of us as well. Help me with my boots; I'm leaving the rest of my clothes on. No telling when I may need to jump up and start shootin' tonight."

"Pray tell, Bill darling, what are you gonna start shootin' at?" I noticed Mary took some stock in what I said and laid her pistol close by her head.

"Two-legged boogers trying to steal the horses tonight."

"Steal our horses, tonight?" Mary questioned, snuggling up to me real close.

"You're dad-burn-tooting, this bunch around here will steal the shirt off your back if you're not watching...just like Susie, someone snatched her right off Main Street, and you and I were practically looking on."

"Tell me about tonight, did you find out anything about Susie's whereabouts?" I thought, at least someone is interested in the poor girl.

"To answer your question, darling, I did find out their method of kidnapping and how they did it so quickly. Do you remember that old hag of a woman sitting in that little nook with curtains on each side of her. . . I'm talking about the one with the crystal ball in front of her, and she had her head tied up with a blue bandana?"

"Oh yes, I remember the old woman, she asked could she give us a free reading, and let us know our fortune. And you said, 'that's a bunch of hog-wash.' I don't believe that is the exact words you used, but she got the message."

"Never mind the exact words. You remember the man that wanted to take our picture free, he was in a tiny, somewhat dim alley way?"

"Yes, I do, he had a handle-bar mustache, and he kept twisting the ends of it."

"You are very observant; this will come in handy tomorrow." Mary had both arms around my neck and her lips touching mine. I could hardly talk.

"What is gonna happen tomorrow, love?"

"We're gonna trap us a rabbit."

"Trap us a rabbit! What in tar-nation do we need with a rabbit tomorrow? I thought we were going to eat at that café downtown on Front Street. Besides, what are we gonna use for bait?"

"You are going to be our bait."

"Me!"

"Yes, listen to what you and I are going to do as soon as the stores open up in the morning... I want you to buy a pair of button up high heel shoes and a young girl's low cut dress. If you will, wear your hair in pigtails, so you will look much younger than you really are."

"You don't want much out of me, do you, baby? And then what do you want me to do for you?"

"First of all, this is for Susie and not for us. When you get all fixed up like a little girl, we will not walk together as we did today, but you will prance along by yourself, hoping to be kidnapped by the same bunch that kidnapped Susie. Let's hope they will take you to the same place they took her. I will be very close, watching you every minute."

"Do you really think this mob will kidnap me like they did Susie?"

"Well, let's hope they do; then I will follow you to where they have Susie locked up."

"You know, Bill darling, this could be dangerous, couldn't it?" I knew now that Mary was a little concerned.

"I think it could be, for anyone that wanted to interfere with their operation, but they don't want to hurt you girls, they want to sell you." I guess these words pacified Mary and she went on to sleep.

The next morning I already had my boots on and was tying my Colt to my leg when Mary woke up. I looked out from under the wagon and saw most of the camp was up, and thank goodness our horses were still here.

"I see the Mason family is up and stirring this morning," I said to Mary. "You stay here and get ready to go in to town I'm going to walk over and talk to the preacher." I could tell they were in the process of fixin' breakfast when I walked up. "I looked for your daughter until late last night." Neither he nor his wife said a word, but kept right on working; he was punching up the fire and she was slicing some salt-back.

"Reverend Mason, you and I had a similar discussion yesterday about your daughter missing. I was hoping maybe you had changed your mind about some things." I was waiting for him to get the fire going and say something, when I noticed several men from the camp approaching me. Mr. Mason eased up from the fire and joined the two men that walked up.

"Can we talk with you, young man?" One of the men asked.

"You sure can, and my name is Bill Allen, and I prefer you address me as Bill. How can I help you this fine mornin'?"

"Well, this is a touchy subject on the part of us all.. Reverend Mason, standing there, tells us how you persuaded the two men to bring back all the stolen provisions he had for the trip out west. We don't cater to that type of ungodly behavior. We trust in the Lord to fight our battles."

"Yes, and one more important thing," the other gentleman began to speak. "Why do you parade around our camp with that deadly weapon strapped to your side? Only desperadoes and outlaws wear these devices." I just stood there listening. without saying a word.

"And another thing, young man, it is called fornication when a man and woman, that is not married, sleeps together." By this time the other two men of the camp had shown up and wanted to put in their two cents.

"Have the other gentlemen mentioned to you about how the young woman you are sleeping with is disgracing our camp, wearing britches like a man in front of our children?"

I was thinking to myself, I am sure glad Mary is over at the buckboard not listing to this rubbish; I was about to get a gut full, myself.

"Has the Reverend Mason told you about his daughter getting kidnapped yesterday, while we were in town?" The men began to look at each other. Then Rev. Mason spoke up: "I've already told our party of believers what happened, how our adopted daughter took the opportunity yesterday to run away from us. Her rebelling spirit overtook her biblical teaching."

"Well, let me tell you body of so called believers, Susie did not run away, she was kidnapped, and is going to be sold to the highest bidder in New Orleans, just as quick as this bunch of sons of a bitch can get her there. And I plan to get her back, if I half to kill every low-life bastard in Vicksburg Mississippi." I quickly turned to walk away.

"Well, don't you bring her demonic molested body back to this camp even if you find her!" Mr. Mason shouted, as I walked away.

I never even looked back. Mary was standing by the wagon when I returned. "Put everything we own in the buck-board, and every thing that belongs to this bunch of religious fruit cakes. . . throw it out on the ground. I'm going to go get the horses; we're leaving this camp right now."

When I returned, I threw the saddles in the wagon and tied our horses behind the buck-board. I hitched the wagon horse between the wagon staves, and we were ready to pull out.

"Where are we going?" Mary asked, holding on to the wagon seat for dear life.

"I'm going out west. . . hold on."

"What about Susie?" Mary yelled.

"No body cares about Susie, why should we?" I scolded.

"Well I do. Stop the wagon, Bill, please stop the wagon, and let's talk." I whipped the wagon off the road into a clump of oak trees, before I got into town.

"Okay, my dear, let's talk!"

"You know, Bill, I love you more than my own life, and I will do anything you say or tell me to do for you, and I would never go against you. But, we're no better than that bunch of religious fanatics we left behind, if we don't try to rescue Susie from her kidnappers."

"I would say that is hitting below the belt, Mary, but you are absolutely right. But we have two problems to contend with, and we can talk about them. First of all, we have all that money in the saddle bags, and there is no way we can leave it unattended, and there is no way I can carry it around with me while I'm looking for Susie."

"You said there are two problems, what is the other one?" Mary asked, getting down out of the wagon.

"That bunch of religious fanatics don't want Susie back, under any circumstances, to defile their camp. That means if we find her ,we will be stuck with her."

"Well, is that so bad? She could be lots of help to us going west," Mary replied

"But we still have the first problem to contend with. . .the horses and wagon and all the money," I said, getting down off the wagon. I looked all around. It was still early and no one was stirring. "The answer is right under our nose, Mary darling."

"It is? I don't feel anything under my nose."

I walked around on the side of the buck-board where Mary was standing, put my arms around her waist, and pulled her very close to me.

"Do you know I love you more today than I loved you yesterday, if that's possible? Let's you and I go down in the woods this morning."

"Oh yes, yes, darling, I would like that very much, but why are you bringing the saddle bags of money?"

"We are going to hide it until we are ready to leave Vicksburg, when ever that will be."

We found the perfect spot, a stump hole beside a big hollow log. I dropped the saddle bags in the stump hole and covered them with straw where no one would ever find them.

"Is that all we are going to do while we are down here in the woods, darling?"

"I guess so, darling, that is unless you had some other plans, like picking some flowers or doing some bird watching," I answered, as I started back out of the woods.

"Oh well, I guess we do have lots to do today." And here she came stompin' right behind me.

"That took care of the money, now the horses and wagon."

"Do you have any ideas atall?" Mary asked, as I started to climb on the buck-board."

"Come on, you'll see."

I popped the whip and headed out to the road toward town. Sitting right before my very own eyes was a livery stable and black smith shop; the problem was solved. I pulled the wagon right up front and eased out of the buck-board. I heard a beating noise inside and knew someone was there. I looked all around and went on in the shop. I guess there was about everything a man could ever need - either hanging up or sprawled out on the saw-dust floor.

The big man, that was beating on a horse shoe, looked up and caught my gaze and threw the horse shoe over in a bucket of water sitting nearby. The middle-aged man very muscled up and had more hair on his chest than I did on my head, and I ain't had a hair cut since I don't know when. He took a few steps my way.

Chapter Eight

"How you wuz, Bill Allen?" Now that set me back on my heels.

"How did you know my name, mister?" He reached down and pulled up his britches revealing a wooden leg.

"Now I know! Frank Mills, I fought with you at the battle of Athens and Decatur. You fought them damn Yankees like tomorrow wasn't coming."

"Still ain't got lots of use for them sons of a bitch, either, although I did marry one. I see you're still wearing that 1851 Navy issue, hanging to your knees. What can I do you out of this morning ‚Bill?"

"I need to leave a buck-board and three horses here for a few days, while I take care of some business."

"Your wish is my command. You got 'em out front?" We walked out front and Frank sized up the situation. "You want me to keep the girl too?" he asked. We both went to laughin', but I don't think Mary thought it was so funny.

"Frank, this is Mary; I drug her over from Alabama. We're going to Texas to get us a ranch, where we're gonna raise babies and long horn cows."

"From what I been reading, if the troops don't get the Redskins under control, you'll be killin' more Indians that we did them damn Yankees. Well, you children go on and do what ever it is you were gonna do today. I'll take over here. And don't worry about your horses."

Mary and I decided to go with Plan A; this is where she would dress like a young girl and try to get kidnapped by the bunch of thugs. Our first stop was the clothing store, where Mary could get her shoes and dress. Next to the beauty parlor, to get her hair put up in pigtails. Mary changed into her dress, put her pants, shirt and boots in a sack, and asked the lady could she hold on to them until later. She told her she would be rewarded.

I'll be the first to admit Mary was being mistaken for my daughter. At the café she and I had a breakfast and dinner rolled into one, not knowing the future of our covert operation. We made other plans just in case Plan A didn't work. There was a lot that could go wrong, and we knew it. After Mary was kidnapped, would I be able to follow her?

"Now, Mary, I don't know when or where you will be apprehended, but I will be close by, you can be sure of that. I will follow you to wherever you are taken...but it may be tonight before I can set you and Susie free."

"I'm ready when you are. You want me to just keep walking up and down Main Street and do everything that might could get me kidnapped?" she asked.

Mary left the café before me, just in case someone was watching us. Of course, I stayed to one side and watched her like a hawk. She was perfect for this job; she went in and out of stores and shops, stopping to window shop at times. I kept a close, but safe distance, and watched closely as she approached the old woman with the crystal ball.

I could tell the old woman said something to Mary, but I couldn't hear what it was. Mary glanced over at me and went over to where the old lady was sitting. She stood for a minute, then sat down at the small table. Immediately the old woman reached to one side, pulled a small rope, and the curtains closed. This, I hadn't planned on. Now I couldn't see either the old woman or Mary. I knew in my spirit this was where she would be kidnapped. I didn't want to blow my cover by running an' snatching the curtain open. She might be reading Mary's fortune.

I guess I stood there for the better part of two minutes trying to make up my mind what to do. Then the curtains began to open up and there sat the old woman, but no Mary. I knew right then they had pulled the wool over my eyes. Using every muscle in my legs, I ran to the back alley of that building, only to see a wagon going around a curve a block away. It was heading in the direction of the big Mississippi River.

I reckoned I ran about as fast as I could, but to no avail. Why the driver of the wagon was in such of a hurry, I don't know? Evidently he knew where he was going; he lost me in the back alleys and slums. I had to slow down and rest. All I had to go on was the fact he was going down to the riverfront. Of course I could always look for a sweaty horse and wagon parked alongside a river boat, or should I say, miles of river boats, every size, shape and model. This was Slumville, if you asked me. Suddenly my luck began to change when I saw this ol' man and woman, sitting on the small porch of a river boat. I stopped - catching my breath.

"Pardon me, Sir, but did you see a horse and wagon pass by here, running lickety-split?"

"We sure did, Sonny, I told Gertrude sittin' here, the damn fool is gonna run that horse in the ground, or turn the wagon over goin' around that curve up yonder," he pointed me toward the curve.

I thanked the man and tore out again, heading for the curve he was talking about. As I rounded the sharp curve, there was still no wagon in sight. But my luck hadn't run out yet, there stood a Black man beside the road, looking up in the air, holding a fishing pole an' bucket.

"Pardon me Sir, but did you see a horse and wagon pass by here running lickety-split?"

"Yes sir, I shore did, the damn fool near run me over; I was just thanking the good Lord he didn't flatten me out." I tore out again thinking to myself. . . is everybody in Vicksburg a damn fool?

I looked up ahead, and there sat,beside the bank of the road, a nearly new, Studebaker, buck-board and a sweaty horse. I stopped and began to catch my breath, trying to stay out of sight, knowing I was at the right place. I made my way through some bushes, over to the bank of the river, and looked toward the houseboat that was tied up. There was a wooden dock that ran from the river bank to the houseboat. Evidently, the man that had brought Mary over had already carried her aboard the houseboat. I could see two men standing on the porch near the dock, talking. Soon, one of the men came back and got in the wagon and left, traveling much slower.

I sat in the underbrush for the better part of an hour, watching. No one came or left. I decided to go with my original plan and come back after dark, bringing the wagon, and a gallon of coal oil, to burn this rat's nest to the water level.

Just as I made my way back to the road, such as it was, I heard a noise and turned my eyes back toward the river. I saw only a small steamboat and didn't think much about it, until I saw it was heading straight for the houseboat. Then the thought hit me like a ton of bricks, this is why the damn fool was driving the wagon so fast, he probably knew this was the day for the boat to come for the girls.

I went back into the bushes to give this some serious thought, if they managed to get the girls loaded on the boat, what was I to do? I certainly couldn't go after them. I had to stop the boat from leaving. As I sat there watching, two men docked the boat beside the houseboat, tied it off, and went inside, carrying a few sacks.

I sat back down in the bushes and put my brain in gear. I couldn't let this boat leave with the girls on board...so how could I keep this from happening? I didn't have many options to choose from: blow it up - I didn't have any explosive; burn it up – it was too close to the houseboat, and the girls might get hurt. My last option was to sink it. But that would involve putting a hole in the boat. Then I remembered, several times I had heard the boat engine popping off steam. That's it, I could fire up the fire box and close the pop off valve. But this now involved getting on board, without being seen.

"What I need is a disguise just in case I get caught. I need to turn myself into a fisherman instead of a gunslinger," I muttered to myself. I had no trouble finding a few fishing poles and worm cans. They were all over the place. I even found a couple of water buckets with holes in the bottom. Now, with the fishing poles, and an arm load of cans and buckets, I started down the long dock toward the boat, like I had good sense. So far so good, I wasn't noticed. I reached the boat and still I hadn't seen anyone. I stepped over onto the boat deck, and started toward the boiler room - still no one. I quickly opened the fire box and threw four or five shovels full of rich, Alabama coal on the simmering fire, and turned off all the relief and safety valves I could lay my hands on. I then picked up my load of fishing poles and buckets and started back toward the bank. As I passed the door to the houseboat, I could her men laughing and swearing. Now I remembered the men carrying several sacks, probably wine and whiskey, if the truth be known. I discarded the poles and buckets and ran for my hide, into the bushes. Black smoke from the boat's boiler was billowing to the high heaven. I wondered if all my work was in vain, as I watched a man come out of the houseboat and look up toward the hill. I know now, he was waiting for the wagon to come back with another girl or two. But they wouldn't be leaving on this steam boat any time soon.

Talk about an explosion - it's hard to explain! It nearly blew my hat off - and the man standing on the porch of the houseboat. - I don't know what happened to him. As far as I know, there were only two men left on the boat; they both ran out to help put out the fire. Naturally, the explosion caused an up stir in the surrounding area, and several men ran over to give a helping hand. I volunteered my help, also; I picked up a piece of one inch pipe, about four feet long, and ran onto the boat to help. I recognized one of the kidnappers, and hit him a lick up about his head and shoulders. Over the side of the boat he went; face down he started his journey to the Gulf of Mexico. I looked through the fire and smoke, and right before my eyes was the other man, dipping up water and throwing it on the burning coals. Without too much fanfare, I gave him a lick right in the face, sending him to keep his buddy company on the way to the Gulf.

Other than the man, blown off the porch by the explosion, the girls were here by themselves. The several volunteers had the fire put out and were leaving, not having a clue about the kidnapping operation and the girls.

With no one around, I opened the door to the houseboat and went inside The girls were unharmed, but locked in a homemade cage. I motioned for the girls to move back. The lock was no match for my piece of four foot iron pipe.

"This is my man," I heard Mary say several times. There were six girls, counting Mary and Susie.

I eased to the door to see if the coast was clear. To my surprise, here came the wagon, and the best I could tell the kidnapper had another very young girl with him. I stood at the door watching him looking at the smoldering boat. Everything else seemed normal as he came down the pier with the girl. I turned to the other girls and told them to stand back. I had already flipped the thong off the hammer of my Colt, and was ready. The door opened and he shoved the girl in, thinking the others were still locked in the houseboat. Then he looked back toward the boat. It gave Mary time to pull the young girl to one side. When the man stepped inside and saw something was wrong, he went for the pistol in his shoulder holster; that was his first mistake. I fanned off three rounds as he staggered back through the door, and we all heard the Mighty Mississippi splash.

"Mary, Darling, tell the girls to get what they want to carry with them, and then run up the pier, and get in the buck-board."

I found three lamps and lanterns in the place, and I began to pour the coal oil all over the floor.

"What are you doing, Bill darling, are you gonna burn the place up?"

"Yes, now you and Susie run and get in the wagon with the others." Mary and Susie ran to the door and stopped and turned back.

"Don't burn up all the money!" Susie exclaimed.

"There is a strong box sitting over in that cabinet; I heard the men say it has lots of money in it!" Mary shouted.

"Well, you and Susie come and get it, because this place is going up in smoke."

It was all they could carry, but up the hill they went. I set fire to the place and headed for the wagon.

"Now you girls keep a low profile, and if you can - lie down in the wagon, or stay covered up, until we can get through town."

For the first time in my life I didn't know what to do. I had a wagon load of girls and nowhere to go. I certainly wasn't going to the so called law in this town, I'm sure this kidnapping operation had roots higher up that we didn't know about.

Mary was sittin' beside me in the wagon, keeping a sharp eye out for danger. I didn't think we had anything to worry about now. All the witnesses had been killed, one way or the other.

"For heaven's sake, Mary, what are we going to do with all these girls?"

"From what I can find out, two of the girls live here in Vicksburg, and can be carried back to their parents. The other two girls have run away from home. They said their parents were mean to them. And you know the story with Susie."

"Yes, and how sad it is! Have you talked to her about her parents? Does she know her folks don't want her back anymore?" I asked, trying to watch the road.

"All I know is. . .the girl is really confused, and this kidnapping has not helped matters at all," said Mary.

"We are going to need a place to stay tonight. We don't have food or enough blankets for all the girls. It does get chilly before morning."

"What about your friend you were in the war with? Maybe he has an idea since he lives here in Vicksburg."

"You're talking about old Frank Mills. That's a good idea. Mary, let's go over there first, besides, we'll be nearly out of town." When the girls and I drove up in front of the blacksmith shop, they had come out of hiding and were looking all around.

"You ladies stay here in the wagon, I'll be right back."

As I walked inside the shop, Frank had just finished another horseshoe and was throwing it in the bucket of water to cool.

"Back so soon?" He asked, and came to me me, kicking up saw dust with that wooden leg. I recollected the night the doctor had to saw his leg off to save his life.

"Come out front, I have something in the wagon I want to show you, Frank." He walked up to the new Studebaker wagon and stared.

"Nice, very nice," he commented, as he surveyed all the young ladies. Then Frank caught my gaze. "How much are you asking fer 'em?" He and I had a good laugh. I went ahead and told Frank the whole story, how Susie was kidnapped from Mary and me while shopping.

"How in the world did you overcome the odds, Bill, this is a closed mouth operation?"

"It's a long story, Frank. I had to kill four men to get the girls to safety. And now I've wound up with no place to go." Frank took a step back and pulled a big red bandanna out of his back pocket and wiped the sweat from his face and neck. He took a step toward the wagon and stuck the bandanna back in his back pocket.

Chapter Nine

"You know I just might have the solution to your problem." Mary quickly slid across the wagon seat near me so as not to miss a word.

"Believe it or not, before the war, and before the town of Vicksburg spread out, and the grazing land grew up with trees, this was a huge ranch. I bought the land here next to the road from old man Picket, God rest his soul. The barn is my livery stable and blacksmith shop. Now I said all of that to say this, behind my shop is the bunk house, which is still in good shape. The last time I looked, it had six or seven bunks. And the pitcher pump, by the sink, still works. To top it all off, it has a fine wood stove, and plenty of wood right at the back door."

"I'll take it sight unseen, Brother Frank."

"Now it might need a smidgen of sweepin' out, but it looks like you have plenty of help."

"You ladies, jump out the wagon and follow the man." It was even in better shape than I first thought, after taking a quick gander. The way the girls went to work, you would have thought we were going to stay here for the duration. Mary quickly made up a list of the things we needed from town. Since the buck-board was already hooked up, and the General Store was not but a hoop and holler down the road, Mary and I headed that way.

Coal oil for the lamps and lanterns and a few more blankets were first on our list. The girls had finished tidying up when we turned to the bunkhouse. They had all voted to have pancakes for supper. I personally think the side of bacon, and that gallon of Blue-Ribbon syrup, was the deciding factor. The girls had dug out plenty of cooking pots and pans, along with two big iron skillets, which were quickly put to good use.

It brought tears to my eyes, the way the young girls were carrying on. The smoked bacon was popping and the aroma of fresh coffee brewing filled the air. And just to think, I had played a part in shaping the way the girls would turn out. I wondered how many had fallen between the cracks and had no one can save them from those butchers.

After supper, the dishes were washed and dried; one of the girls put on another pot of coffee. I sat on one of the bunks while all the girls sat around the table with their cups of coffee, telling their life stories. Mary started first, and told how her pa went off to war and never came back, then a year later her mom died and left her to fend for herself.

"Then, Bill, sitting over there," she looked over my way, "came riding up, and I took a shot at him." All the girls went to laughin'.

"When my knight in shining armor shows up, I don't think I will shoot at him," one of the girls said.

As I sat there sipping on my coffee, I heard some sad tales along with the good. Some told how their parents loved them, while others told how their dads had beaten them.

They all had the same story: how the old woman with the crystal ball tricked them, and they were hurried off to the houseboat. Mary explained to the young girls what would have happened if the boat had picked them up and carried them to New Orleans. One could hear the oohs and aahs around the table. Finally, the coffee was gone and everyone was sleepy. I let the ladies have the bunks, and I made me a pallet at the far end of the bunk house.

I was wakened the next morning, by Frank milling around in the blacksmith shop. I slipped on my boots,my gun rigging down, eased over to the kitchen sink, and started pumping water for coffee. The sun was shining through the few windows in the small building. Soon the girls began yawning, and all eased up to get coffee.

I knew some decisions had to be made today, so I put my thinking cap on, and began to think. I knew two of the girls lived in Vicksburg and could be carried back home. That left the two runaways - I was not sure if I knew what to do. They were older, but there was no way they could take care of themselves in the transition the North and

South was having. As far as Susie was concerned, I was going to take her back to the wagon train and try to explain what had happened hoping, maybe, the preacher would have had a change of heart.

It seemed the girls were having fun this morning, stirring up breakfast. There was a boiler of grits bubbling on the stove, eggs were being cracked and smoked bacon being sliced. I was hankering to get hold of one of Mary's cat head biscuits, and some of that Blue-Ribbon syrup.

After breakfast I tried to explain to the girls how this should be a learning experience for them: I had to kill four men to get them set free, and I could be in big trouble, as of right now.

"I hope you all know, if the right men found out what I did to save you, it would be Katie bar the door. Ladies, remember, nothing is free. Watch who you trust, the rest of your lives." They all nodded and agreed that they would.

"Now, Betty Sue, you said you were in town with your mother when you were kidnapped. . . and you know where you live. . .we will carry you home first. I know your parents are worried sick and probably have gone to the sheriff by now. Debby, you can be next. You said you were in town with your family and the same thing happened to you. I tell you what I'm gonna do. . .I think before I leave Vicksburg, I will pay the witch behind the crystal ball a visit." I could tell the girls were in full agreement.

"Now you two ladies that ran away from home, - what are your plans since you are free again?"

Dorothy spoke up first, with some regret in her voice, "I might have been better off to have stayed at home and tried to make a go of it."

"That goes for me, as well," Ruby replied.

"Well, do you girls want to go back home and try it again? I can't make up your mind for you!"

"Could you give us some time to think about it?"

"Oh yes, you two stay here with Susie, while me and Mary carry Debby and Betty Sue home." And within the hour we had the two girls with their families, safe and sound. Mary and I did our best explaining what had happened to their daughters and how we were glad we could help.

When Mary and I arrived back at the bunk house, Ruby and Susie were all upset, almost in tears. "Mr. Bill, there was nothing we could do to change Dorothy's mind; she struck out on her own, in spite of everything we could do or say."

"Oh well, we can't win 'em all, try is all we can do. Would you two ladies look under that far bunk, and bring me the strong box we took from the boat house, before I burned it up?"

The ladies did what I asked and set it on the table in front of me. I had gone by the blacksmith shop and borrowed a rather large pry bar from Frank ,to pry the box open. We had no idea what we would find, only that the men on the houseboat said it contained a right smart amount of money. Well, when it was opened were we surprised! Now we knew why the metal box was so heavy. It was more money than I wanted to count, right then. I did give each of the girls two hundred dollars, and I hid the strong box, until we would come back.

"Come on! I'm carrying you ladies out to lunch today. We will eat at the café and then carry Susie home." The girls spread a blanket in the wagon to sit on, and we were on our way.

"Mr. Bill, this is more money than I have ever seen, is it really mine?" Ruby asked, holding up the hundred dollar bills.

"Yes! It's all yours, to spend anyway you want to, but I'm buying dinner." I noticed Susie wasn't saying much.

'Susie, are you not feeling well?' I asked, as we ate.

"Oh, Mr. Bill I'm feeling quite well, and thank you for the money. I'm going to buy me a new dress all of my own."

"Do you want to share anything with us, Susie?" Mary asked.

"Well, yes and no," Susie paused..."I'm not the lily white, little thirteen year-old virgin everyone thinks I am." She hung her head and laid her fork down by her plate and wiped her mouth. "I was eight years old when my uncle and Aunt Grace adopted me from his older sister, which was my mother. I never knew my daddy. For the five years I've lived with my uncle and aunt, I have called them Mother and Father; and they let on to all their friends I was their daughter. All the time I lived with them, all I have ever known, and all they have ever talked about - was my mother being a bar-room slut. I think she is dead now."

"Are you saying you don't want to go back and live with them?" Mary asked, as she laid her hand on the back of Susie's hand.

Susie hung her head, "you want the whole story?"

"Not really, Susie, save yourself from the embarrassment. Me and Bill have read between the lines...it's not my britches that upsets your uncle, the preacher man. He wants to get in my britches. It's not your demonic spirit he can't get control over, it's the demonic spirit between his legs he can't get control over." I sat there listening to the girls talk, thinking, there just isn't any good in some folks atall.

"You see, I was nearly nine years old when Aunt Grace and Uncle Terry took me from his sister to live with them. They didn't have any children at the time. It was whispered through the church that Uncle Terry couldn't have children, and he had been married to Aunt Grace for eight years. As I was saying, I'm neither saint, nor am I a dumb little thirteen year old girl, either. My Uncle Terry claims to be a preacher, and I knew he and I were doing things I was not supposed to do. And the way my uncle explained it to me, it seemed all right in the sight of God. He even told me that Aunt Grace didn't want him to bother her, and God sent me to him. . .he even had Bible scripture for all of this....until Aunt Grace had the first child. Then, after the second baby came, he and Aunt Grace began to despise me. During Aunt Grace's two pregnancies, my uncle wanted to have sex almost every night with me. In the last year, he became very bold and not very cautious, and Aunt Grace caught us twice. The first time she couldn't believe her eyes, and Uncle Terry lied his way out of having had sex with me. The second time Aunt Grace caught him, she started packin' up to leave, and he fed her another lie, and said I had a demonic Jezebel spirit in me, and he would pray that I would leave and never come back, or die. Since then I had been staying pretty much to myself - until the day we were robbed, and you and Mary came along."

"Well if that don't beat it all. I have a good mind to go over there and punch that hypocrite bastard right in the nose." I looked over at Ruby, tears were streaming down her face.

"I guess sad stories like this makes you cry, like me." Mary said, wiping tears from her own eyes. Then Ruby really broke down. Susie eased up from the table, went around behind Ruby, and put her arms around her neck trying, to console her. Mary handed her a napkin to dry her eyes.

Ruby begin to speak through trembling lips, "Susie just told my story, only it was my father. I had an older sister, Macy, and she committed suicide. Like Susie's uncle, my father had an excuse; my mother was always sickly. After she died last month, my own daddy had what he always wanted; my sister was gone and my mom was out of the way. The first night it was hell on this earth; my daddy went crazy drinkin', and tore all my clothes off. . .and the rest wasn't fun. I even thought about killin' him. I just had to leave home! He finally passed out and I ran...and wound up in Vicksburg. "

It took all I could do to keep from bursting out crying, in the café, right in front of the girls, with other people watching, too.

"Are you ladies ready to go? I just want to shoot something, or somebody. Mary, Darling, if you have a story like these girls, just keep it to yourself, until later."

"No, Darling, I only had one man who wanted to dance with me, and you shot him dead." That cheered the girls up, and we all eased up to leave the café.

When we approached the buck-board to leave, Susie said. "Did he really do that?"

"Do what?" Mary questioned, getting in the wagon.

"Did Mr. Bill shoot the man that asked you to dance?"

"You're darn-tooting, and shot his brother too!"

"Well, he surely doesn't seem like a bad sort, does he, Ruby?"

"No, he doesn't, but did you see what he did to the fellow at the houseboat?"

"Yeah, Mr. Bill filled him so full of lead ,he sunk like a horseshoe when he hit the water."

"What are you girls yakking about back there?" I asked.

"We're talking about how nice you are, and how good looking you are."

"Yes, and how lucky Mary is to have a man like you to take care of her," said Ruby.

"You ladies haven't noticed that she takes care of me? Get Mary to tell you how she broke me out of jail one night, over in the town of Evart, Alabama."

"Don't forget to pull over to the clothing store, and let me get my britches and boots that I left there the day I bought this dumb dress."

"You need to let Susie and Ruby go in and get rigged out with some boots, jeans, and a hat, we are heading out west in the mornin'."

While I was sitting in the wagon in front of the clothing store, I put on my thinking cap and began to size the situation up. What would we need to get to the wild, wild West, comfortably? How would we carry what we would need for the trip? I was sure we could stop along the way and pick up some supplies as needed. Next I would need a way to get us from here to there - a covered wagon and a good team of horses. Since the war, those had been in short supply.

But with the money from the bank robbery, I had buried, and the money from the houseboat, I could buy Vicksburg, Mississippi and most of the folks that lived here. Oh well, I'll talk it over with the girls and see what they think.

"It looks like you ladies bought them out," I said, as the ladies were returning to the wagon.

"Not quite, how do you like our cowgirl hats?" They all smiled real big, and modeled their new hats.

"Now if y'all ain't somethin'."

"You ought to see our boots and britches, Mr. Bill. Just look, we're real cowgirls going out west with you."

"What do you ladies think about us buying a big covered wagon to go out west in?"

Chapter Ten

The vote was unanimous, and the girls were tickled to death. Sleeping on the cold ground with the snakes wasn't their cup of tea.

"Well y'all load up, time's a wasting. Let's look for a covered wagon." My first stop was the livery and blacksmith shop. I had no trouble finding Frank. I just followed the noise of the pounding hammer. I walked in on his blind side and startled him, when he turned around.

"Good lord, man, you need to make some noise when you sneak in here on me!" We both started laughing.

"Tell me something Frank, where would a person going out west find a prairie schooner, or maybe a Conestoga? It would be much larger."

"I can see you want all the comforts of home with a Conestoga wagon. And with the four of you going west I can see why. To tell you the truth, Bill, there are plenty of wagons in Vicksburg for sale, but the animals to pull the wagons are in short supply."

"I know what you mean. The South army commandeered so many of the farm horses, and the North literally confiscated what they needed when they were burning and killing," I spat out. Just talking about it made me mad.

"Well now, Bill, before you get all bent out of shape and want to start shootin' your Colt...there is a farm about four miles up Brady Road where you can probably buy a team of good horses."

"What about a wagon?"

"I think ol' man Dickman will have just what you want, he dabbles in new and used wagons and will probably have a Conestoga over there."

"You want to ride over to his place early tomorrow and help me out? You know wagons and horse flesh a whole lot better than I do."

"Now I don't mind if I do, at least it would give my arm a rest."

It was getting late and the girls had gone over to the bunk house to try on their new clothes and start supper. I had put in my order for pancakes again; one of the trio sure knew how to make up flap-jack batter. I hung around the blacksmith shop until Frank closed up for the night, then went on home. As I eased on over to the bunkhouse, I could smell the bacon frying and the coffee brewing.

Now you talking about a sight for sore eyes, these girls were decked out in boots and britches and flipping pancakes up to the ceiling! Susie brought me a cup of coffee and I sat down and watched as they set the table.

"You know you two ladies are gonna make some men fine wives."

Ruby placed a plate down in front of me as she set the table. "Do you think I'm too young to get married, Mr. Bill?"

"I don't know. How old are you?" I asked as I squared my chair around at the table. "I have no earthly idea. . .you look old enough to marry."

"Well I'm glad you think so! I'm only sixteen- years old," Ruby said, strutting back over where Mary was putting butter between the hotcakes.

"What about me, Mr. Bill, I would make a man a good wife don't you think?" Susie said, twisting around in her rather tight britches.

I was just a little embarrassed at the girls. "You ladies are gonna get me in trouble before I eat my supper. But I do know out west ladies get married at an early age."

Mary brought the pancakes over and set them on the table and proclaimed, "I'm only seventeen, and Bill and I are going to get hitched as soon as we can find a real preacher."

As the four of us sat and talked after supper, sipping on a fresh pot of coffee, I shared some thoughts with the girls concerning our trip out west; how each one of us would need to carry our own load. "First I'm going to make sure you ladies are going to know how to load a gun and shoot...and hit what you are shootin' at."

I told the girls it would be close quarters for a lengthy time. The inside of a pioneer wagon, or Conestoga wagon as they were often called, was designed first for utility and then for comfort. We'd need to pack enough supplies to last the four of us for up to six months, into an area usually ten feet long and four feet wide.

"This will be your job before we leave Vicksburg," I instructed them. "While Frank and I go look for the wagon and horses tomorrow, you ladies make a list of everything we will need to carry on our trip out west."

It was a beautiful morning when I awakened. The girls were ready to get their list started and had breakfast almost ready. I went through my usual routine: boots, gun belt, and hat. . .no I didn't forget my britches, I slept in 'em. Frank already had our horse saddled and ready to ride by the time I walked over to the livery stable.

"I thought you were gonna sleep all day," Frank joked. The sun had just come over the trees when Frank and I mounted and started east, toward the ol' Brady road.

Now I didn't know at the time that we had to go right by where Mr. Mason and the four other men had their wagons parked. Frank and I were getting caught up on war stories and reminiscing about the times he and I had in service. As we passed, I cut an eye toward the wagons....instead of four wagons there were five in the circle. I also noticed there were some horses missing.

"Frank," I said, "This is the bunch of religious fanatics I rode into town with. I see the wagons, but over half of the horses are missing."

"Well, if they didn't keep an eagle eye on 'em, somebody made off with them right under their noses."

"If we got a few minutes, let's stop and see why they haven't started out west yet." Frank and I turned off the road and started toward the wagons. I saw Mrs. Mason, along with her two children, hanging some clothes on a temporary clothesline that ran from the wagon to a small tree near by.

"Good morning, Mrs. Mason," I said, halting my horse and looking around. She turned from the clothesline and walked my way.

"If you're looking for Terry, he's not here."

"No I wasn't looking for the preacher. I just noticed when Frank and I was passing it looked like some of the horses were missing."

The two children walked up by her side and she put her hand on their shoulder.

"Yes, someone slipped into camp last night and two teams of eight horses were stolen."

"Where is the preacher?," I asked. "Is he out looking for the thief that swiped your horses?" I noticed that Mrs. Mason seemed to not be too concerned about the missing horses.

"No! He's down in the woods praying that whoever took them will soon bring them back."

"Your husband is a damn fool, Mrs. Mason. Your team could be headed for Louisiana right now."

"I know it, Mr. Bill, that's why I'm leaving him this morning," she said, pulling the two small children close to her side."

"What you do is all up to you, Mrs. Mason. But, did you know we got Susie back unharmed?" A smile came on Mrs. Mason's face.

"I know her real father will be glad to hear the good news."

"You're telling me you know who Susie's real daddy is? I knew she knew who her mother was....she told us the other night. She said the preacher told her that her mother was a slut, and threw it up to her every day."

"My husband was right about that in some ways." She looked down at the young boy and girl standing by her side. "Garry, you and Jill run over there and play. I want to talk to Mr. Bill this morning." The children quickly ran back to play in the sand. "Let me quickly start at the beginning, Susie was eight years old when her mother, my husband's sister, Yvonne, she just up and disappeared into thin air. Course the war was going on and Susie's daddy was in the war, and not at home at the time. She comes up missing. To make this story shorter, my husband Terry and I had been married about seven or eight years and had no children. Now there was nothing to do but for my husband and me to take Susie in and care for her. We lived in Brewton, Alabama at the time and my husband was very involved in his church work. Now let me tell you 'bout Arthur Gates. . . he was a loner, but a good man. He got involved with my husband's sister and the church. Eight years before Yvonne disappeared, Susie was born. No one knew who the daddy was because Yvonne was the town whore, and would lay with anybody. And no one ever suspected Arthur Gates being involved, him being in the church and all."

"You are going to tell me the new wagon in the circle belongs to Arthur Gates?" Mrs. Mason looked somewhat surprised at my question.

"Yes, and he is the father of my two children playing over there in the sand. My husband is sterile and has never been able to have children, and thank God, or Susie would have been pregnant ten times. It's sad to say, but Susie clung to my husband like a tick on a dog's ear. And it seemed Terry couldn't keep his hands off her. My husband had nothing to do with me, after Susie came to stay. This is when he persuaded Arthur Gates to have sex with me in order to have a child. Terry said it was very biblical, and showed us where Abraham took a concubine, and had a child. Well, I was young at the time and believed this foolishness, and in nine months we had the girl. We named her Jill, then soon after, he and I had the boy. I managed to get a letter off to Arthur, and told him about Terry and Susie. Just in time don't you think?"

Just before I had time to answer Mrs. Mason's question, a shot rang out from down in the woods where the preacher was supposed to be praying.

"My lord, lady, you suppose that was your husband?" I asked, as I dismounted.

"Oh no! Terry doesn't own a gun."

By this time, Frank had slid out of the saddle, and he and I were heading in the direction of the single shot. Now what we ran in on was a sad sight to say the least. There was Clement Dawkins standing over Mr. Mason with a smoking pistol. Well, it was for certain the preacher had preached his last sermon; Clement Dawkins had put a round ball right between his eyes. As far as Frank and I were concerned, it was an open and shut case. There stood Clement Dawkins mentally disturbed, deaf and dumb daughter, Missy Dawkins. She was staring out into space, without a stitch of clothes on.

By this time, two more of the men from the camp had shown up. I guess the old phrase that was coined years before, 'a picture is worth a thousand words' said it all. Frank looked at me, and I caught his gaze.

"Are you ready to ride, Bill ol' boy? It looks like God took care of this problem."

As we neared the ranch that Frank was telling me about, he began to talk. "The Lord works in mysterious ways, don't you think?"

I didn't know if Frank was talking about what had just happened, or something in his life.

"Yes he does, it looks like this farmer has a lot full of horses."

We saw three men standing at a barn between the house and the horse lot. We rode over to where they were standing. Frank and I saw they were finishing up a business transaction an' stood aside, until the owner of the horse farm finished. I could tell there was some discrepancy over a bill-of-sale.

"Look, gentlemen, any time I buy eight horses I need a bona fide bill-of-sale; I don't want to get in trouble with the Law."

All of a sudden I could feel my bristles rising on my back.

"Mr. Spivey, I didn't think you had to have a bill-of-sale if you were selling your own horses," one of the men said.

"Well, you don't, Jake, but I've been knowin' your pa for years, and he ain't never raised any horse flesh like them eight horses standing over there."

"Mr. Spivey, you ain't calling me and Clem liars, are ya?"

"No! He's calling you two, low-life bastards horse thieves." I knew this statement would cause a stir. I had already flipped the thong off the hammer of my Colt and planted my feet when Jake spun around facing me.

"Boy, you done let your mouth overload your ass." Old Jake went to backing up. "Help me out here, Clem; this boy needs to mind his own business."

"This is my business. You stole those horses not more than six miles from here. And to make matters worse you stole them from a preacher."

"Billy boy, I ain't wearing no gun, you got 'em all by yourself!" Frank said, and he and Mr. Spivey stepped aside. I just figured Jake was the faster of the two, so when his hand moved, I drew and fanned two chunks of lead in his direction, then quickly whipped to favor ol' Clem, and gave him the same treatment, not showing any partiality. Neither man had even cleared leather.

"That's some mighty fine shooting, young man, if I do say so myself."

"My name is Bill Allen, and I'm sure you know my friend Frank Mills. He is owner of the blacksmith shop in Vicksburg."

"Yes, he and I have met several times. I'm always needing a little blacksmith work done."

"Did you say you knew the young men's daddy?" I asked.

"Yes I did, fine old church going man, but always had trouble with Jake and Clem as long as I can remember; always trying to make a fast buck without working for it."

"The reason I'm here this morning is to see if you have a team of good horses to pull a covered wagon for us going out west. But seeing that God works in mysterious ways, I need to take the eight horses, standing over there, back to the original owners, if you have no objection. Frank will vouch for me."

"By all means, get 'em off my property. I don't want any trouble with the Law, such as we have. I will tell one of my farm hands to run over to the dead boys' house to tell their pa he needs to come get them."

As we started back to the camp with the horses, I told Frank how much I appreciated him coming over and showing me the way to the horse farm this morning. I also told him I was going to join up with the wagon train and go west.

Chapter Eleven

By the time Frank and I had brought the horses back to camp, things were pretty much settled down. I learned that someone had said a few words over Mr. Mason, and buried him right where he was lying. Mrs. Mason never told the young children what happened, nor let them go down into the woods where he fell. Mrs. Mason and Arthur Gates had managed to get together, and were loading her, and the children's, belongings into his wagon.

I thanked Frank, my old war buddy, again for going with me this morning, and apologized for the killing. We shook hands and I told him, as he started on back to the blacksmith shop, if he saw any of the girls at the bunk house to tell them I was heading back soon, and to have the list of supplies ready so we could go shopping.

I stayed long enough to talk with the rest of the men from the wagon train. Even Mrs. Mason consented gracefully to my taking her wagon and team of horses for the trip out west. The other families had no problems with me wearing a pistol, or Mary, her britches. That wasn't the only meeting we had before we left for the western territory and it wouldn't be the last. We found out real fast, a wagon train wasn't for a bunch of complainers and lazy folks.

We had problems even before we started and crossed the mighty Mississippi. Most of the horses weren't trained to pull a wagon, let alone pull together in a team effort. We needed to make sure every wagon was well stocked. Arthur Gates actually took on the lead as wagon master. He seemed to have a level head on his shoulders.

Many of the wagons were very poorly stocked with food supplies, and the women did not know how to ration them properly. The labor involved in preparing for a journey west was generally divided equally between women and men. The men loaded the wagons and prepared the livestock, while the women prepared and stocked food and clothing for the journey, as well as deciding what household essentials to pack.

We all outfitted our wagons with a minimum of space and maximum storage in mind. Most of the men took note of how Mr. Clement Dawkins prepared his wagon for the journey. He and Mrs. Dawkins were the couple with the sickly daughter. He showed the other men how to build a box at the front of the wagon, on which to sit while driving. It also had room to store bacon, salt and other supplies inside. The top of the box was made with holes in each corner; it could be lifted off and used as a table, when sharpened sticks were inserted into the holes for legs.

Mrs. Dawkins was no stranger to knowing how to pack a wagon for travel. The women filled an old chest with clothing and other items for use along the way.

She said to the ladies, "We will start out wearing some old clothes , and when we can't wear them any longer we will leave them on the road." She even showed some of the women how cutting material beforehand would save room in packing; others carried bolts of uncut cloth, to be prepared to meet whatever need might arise. Before the journey began, most every woman washed and packed everything suitable to carry on the trip.

The clothing chest was packed in behind the food storage box, and to keep it from slipping around in transit, Mr. Dawkins fastened a system of cleats to the bottom of the wagon bed. Then he put in a chair to ride in, leaving a small space on the floor for their daughter to occupy. After that another trunk containing dishes (most likely china) and household goods set aside for use when they reached their destination, was placed inside. A washtub, and a basket containing the dishes she planned to use on the trip (most likely tin), were stowed in a corner. Then Mr. Dawkins loaded four 125 lb. sacks of flour and one of corn meal, then bags of dried apples and peaches, beans, rice, sugar and coffee.

The morning we planned to move out, we had all had finished packing the wagons. They really looked professional. The nice white covers were drawn down tight to the side boards. We had left a good ridge to keep them from sagging. The cover was high enough for me to stand up straight under the roof, with a curtain to put down in front and another at the back end. The ladies took note how Mrs. Dawkins had finished packing. Her iron ware was stashed in a box that hung outside the wagon, while her butter churn sat by the washtub. When all was packed and ready, she added a feather mattress and pillows, with two comforters on top, which would be laid on top of the boxes and over a side of shoe leather at night.

The ladies spent the last few days before our departure from Vicksburg making provisions to get them through the first week of travel - baking bread, frying doughnuts, stewing dried fruit and cooking a chicken and a ham. I had, unbeknownst to anyone including Mary, built a false bottom in one of the boxes I put in our wagon. This is where I secretly put the money from the bank robbery, and the money we took from the houseboat, before I burned it down.

The first morning we lined up to pull out heading west was a glorious occasion. First of all, everything would be new; we would see things and sights we had never before encountered. The whole wagon train seemed to be in one accord on all major issues, such as religion, and men toting guns, and girls wearing britches.

Mr. Arthur Gates and Mrs. Mason with the young girl and boy, volunteered to take the lead; he was well educated and knew how to read a map. Following up in second place was Mr. and Mrs. Hicks; he also claimed to be a preacher, but kept what he believed to himself. I think after Mr. Mason was shot and killed, it brought a lot to light about "holy men", because Mr. Mason was supposed to have been his best friend.

Getting in line third was Mr. Clement Dawkins, his wife Sarah, and their sickly daughter Missy (who at times would become disoriented and need a right smart of attention.)

In the fourth wagon was Jessie and Julie Parks, a fairly young couple from Bessemer, Alabama. She was about five month pregnant, and hoping to reach their destination before the baby came.

Last, but not least, and bringing up the rear, was our wagon. The girls were already starting to complain that they would be eating dust all the way to wherever we were going.

Susie was introduced to her real daddy, Arthur Gates, and was told the truth that Jill and Garry, the young children, were her half sister and brother. I think she thought a prayer had been answered when the pervert, Mr. Mason, was put to rest; I know there was no love lost with her or Grace his wife.

On the 23rd day of August, in the year 1866, we pulled out on the road east of Vicksburg, Mississippi and headed south about twenty miles to cross the mighty Mississippi River. It was almost dark when the ferry boat took the last wagon across. Arthur Gates found a level spot of ground, and had the wagons to circle for the night. It wasn't a huge circle, there weren't enough wagons; but we did the best we could with what we had. A bonfire was built in the center of the circle, and the ladies started supper. Some felt the biggest challenge of our journey was crossing the mighty Mississippi. But what we didn't know was that we would face a challenge every hour of every day.

Mrs. Dawkins knew Missy, her daughter, wasn't feeling well and helped her plate with food and carried it over to their wagon. We all noticed that Mrs. Dawkins soon came back to the camp fire, with the plate of food untouched.

"Is anything wrong?" Grace asked. She was sitting the closest.

Mrs. Dawkins just stood there, as if she was paralyzed. "Missy is not in the wagon."

I guess it upset the girls the most. They were already finished eating and ran to the Dawkins wagon and began to call out for Missy. Sad to say, this was causing a stir in the whole camp. Everyone had a theory or an idea what had happened to Missy. It was nearing midnight and Missy was nowhere to be found.

What was on everyone's mind, but no one ever mentioned. . . we were camped on the bank of the mighty Mississippi. . .did Missy get out of the wagon unnoticed and walk down to the bank of the raging river?

"Lets all try to get some sleep!" Arthur Gates shouted to everyone. "We'll start the search at break of day."

I'm sure it was a long night for the Dawkins. A thought kept bombarding my mind as I tried to go to sleep. 'The Lord works in mysterious ways'. Was the Lord giving the Dawkins a new start? I do know the daughter was their life; they had no life of their own waiting on Missy hand and foot.

The sun was glitterin' through the trees the next morning as Mary and I saddled our horses. Neither one of us had any idea how far Missy might have walked during the night. I was pulling my cinch strap tight when I heard Susie and Ruby cry out. Well, Mary and I left the horses and ran as fast as we could to the bank of the river. We found Susie and Ruby standing there, looking on in tears. There, for the camp to see, were Missy's dainty silk slippers, with her pink comb lying across them.

I didn't say anything, but I knew this ended the search for Missy. By now Mr. And Mrs. Dawkins had walked up, holding hands. They looked up into the air, said something under their breath, and turned to leave.

"Do you want her slippers, Mrs. Dawkins?" Ruby asked.

Mrs. Dawkins stopped and turned back, "No, just leave them sitting there."

By the time we all had regained our composure and made it back to camp, the Dawkins had harnessed up their wagon and were ready to go west. As far as I know, Missy's name was never mentioned the rest of the trip.

Course now, Mary and I would bring up the subject between us now and then.

Mary said, "It was like a heavy load was taken off their shoulders when Missy drowned herself."

"How can you say such a thing, my dear?" I asked. "They loved their daughter."

"I know, I know, Bill darling, that is why the Dawkins had such a peace giving her up. Don't you think God can do a much better job raising an invalid child than we can?"

"I'm gonna have to chew on that for a while," I said.

We didn't cover much territory that day because of all the excitement. Most everyone in the wagon train seemed to take Missy's drowning hard, and wanted to show respect to the Dawkins in the loss of their daughter. On the bright side, the horses were calmed down and stayed in line. And every one knew his or her place and what to do when we made camp for the evening.

The next day went well; we started early with a good breakfast. It never fails, for me a full stomach always makes the day go better. The girls were in the back of the wagon and had begun their studies. As good fortune would have it, Susie had an extremely good education and was teaching Mary and Ruby how to read and write. Thank goodness, that got me off the hook. I had promised Mary I would teach her to read.

The wagons were spaced out just right, and no one was having to contend with the dust problem from the wagon in front. It ain't much to do just sitting on a seat in the front of a wagon, holding the reins of four horses. It had become ol' school for the horses; they had learned to follow the wagon in front of them.

I was dozing in and out and listening to the girls in back, giggling and carrying on. Was that a whistle I heard? I quickly looked all around and saw or heard nothing. About the time the thought of - had I heard a whistle or was I just hearing things, there it went again. The sound seemed to be coming from behind the wagon. The girls had the flap up in the back of the wagon to get some fresh air. When I turned around and looked back, there was a man standing right in the middle of the road, more or less jumping up and down waving his arms at me.

I pulled the horses to a stop and waited as he ran to catch up to the wagon. You might say, when I stopped and the young man came running up to the wagon, it broke the concentration of reading, writing and arithmetic. The wagons in front of us didn't hear or see the young man as he approached our wagon, and slowly moved on ahead.

"How about catching a ride with you into the next town, mister, I see you have two horses tied behind the wagon?" the good looking young man asked. He was huffing and puffing and slam out of breath.

"Just climb up here with me, the horses don't cotton to strangers ridin' them all that well." He climbed aboard, I popped the reins, and we were on our way. Susie and Ruby were all ears, and was right behind me and the young man, trying to catch every word.

"Say you're going on into the next town, how far is that?" I asked, because Mr. Gates had the map.

"I'm not sure, my name is Ray Colter, and I'm not from around here."

"Well, ain't you a long way from anywhere? We haven't seen or passed a house since we broke camp this morning. You didn't just fall out of the sky, did you?" I asked. Susie and Ruby thought that was funny, I heard them snicker under their breath.

"Oh no, sir, there was a house just off the road, it was back in the woods a ways. That's where I spent the night last night."

I didn't say anything but was more confused now than I had been before. Here was a nice young man, no older than me, all clean and well shaved, in the middle of North Louisiana hitching a ride into the next town; and he didn't even know where it was.

"Well, Bill, you did say your name was Bill, didn't you?"

"I never did say, you heard one of the girls call me Bill, but go on with your story."

"As I was saying, I spent the night with Widow Jones last night, as a matter of fact I spent the whole week with her, ever since she picked me up in town a week ago. Like I started to say, Bill, it's a long story." The young man started grinning like a Chihuahua trying to pass a peach seed.

"We've still got five hours of sun left, and nothing to do but listen to your story, ain't that right, girls?" By now Susie and Ruby was practically slobbering over the young man.

"I was with my Uncle Tom Colter in town when the Widow Jones hired me to help her out with her ranch. She had enlightened me on the money issue, said it wouldn't be much pay, but the fringe benefits would be out of this world." He stopped and licked his lips. "I wonder if I could bother y'all for a drink of water?" Susie and Ruby nearly broke their necks trying to be the first to hand Ray the water jug. I wasn't looking, but I think it was a tie, and they both handed Ray the demijohn with the corncob for a stopper.

The young man took the jug, removed the corncob, took a big slug, and wiped his mouth on his sleeve. I watched as he popped the corncob back in the jug and turned half way around and offered it back to Susie and Ruby. Again, with big cow eyes, they reached for the demijohn.

"Thank you very much ladies, that was very sweet of you, and I believe that was the best drink of water I have ever drank."

"I am so glad you enjoyed it. So Ray, if there is anything else you need, just let me know," Susie replied.

"That goes for me, too," said Ruby, in a soft loving voice.

"Could we get back to the story of the Widow Jones?"

"The rest of the story about Widow Jones...As it turned out, she wasn't no widow. And when her husband showed up this morning toting a double barrel shotgun, I had to run for my life."

"Now if you had to run for your life, why hasn't he caught up with you by now - and you on foot?" I asked.

"You see, his hired stable boy spilled the beans when Mr. Cary showed up this morning. He told his boss all about his wife and me being together, while he was gone to buy a bull last week," the young man paused to catch his breath. "I'm gonna need another swig of that water before I finish the story about Widow Jones." We went through the same routine, and Ray drank his fill and handed the jug back.

"Where was I at in the story?" he asked, wiping his mouth on the back of his hand.

"The husband was coming in the house toting a double barrel shotgun to shoot your ass off."

"Oh yes, I remember now, I was about to get my ass shot off. . . Well, I wasn't on foot when I first started; I ran out the back door , jumped on a good horse that could run, an' I struck out."

"Do you think he is after you now?" I asked.

"Yes sir-ree, but he is chasing a horse without a rider, I was far enough ahead and swung up on a limb, until he passed by." I thought to myself, that was a pretty smart move.

"His stable boy told me when I arrived, that old man Cary was a very jealous and overbearing man, and he had done shot two men for fooling with his young wife. I don't even own a gun."

All of a sudden the wagon in front of me stopped, so I pulled up and stopped, too, and being somewhat cramped, I jumped down on the ground to stretch my legs. I walked up to the wagon in front of me and asked Jessie did he know why we had stopped.

"All I know, Bill, is Mr. Clement Dawkins yelled back here and said a man and a boy was looking in every wagon for a young man."

I was still standing talking to Jessie and his wife when, who I took to be, old man Cary and his stable boy rode by and looked into every wagon. I knew my wagon was next and determined I would let nature take its course. Ray, whatever he said his name was, had made his bed and he could sleep in it. When I got back to my wagon there was no sign of Ray. Old man Cary and his stable boy were heading down the road from where we had just come.

Chapter Twelve

"What happened to Ray?" I asked, climbing back on the wagon.

"He jumped off the wagon and ran, to get away from that old man that was going to shoot his ass off," Ruth said.

"That's right, the old man was going to shoot him," said Susie as she eased up behind the front seat beside Ruby.

"You don't mind if I keep you company for a spell?" Mary asked, climbing between Susie and Ruby in order to sit on the front seat. I guess the wagon train had gone about five or six miles without anyone saying much at all; that was not like this bunch of women.

Mary spoke up first. "You girls... need to tell Bill the truth about Ray, before he smothers to death back there under all those quilts and blankets."

"Mr. Bill, we just couldn't let Ray get shot full of holes."

"That's right, Mr. Bill, we're so sorry, but we just couldn't sit by and let Ray get shot dead, could we?"

"Well, I can't much blame you ladies, ol' man Cary don't need to be out shooting somebody. The old man needs to go home and take care of his wife. Now what are you two girls gonna do with Ray?"

"Well, first I think we need to give him a good talking to, don't you think so Susie?" Ruby suggested.

"I sure do, Ruby, if Mr. Bill will let Ray stay on the wagon train, I believe we can break him from his riotous living."

I didn't say anything at the time, but this was the pot calling the kettle black or the blind leading the blind.

For the next day things ran as smooth as clock work, and speaking of work, Susie and Ruby had put Ray in charge of the ax. It was his job to see that the wagon train had wood for the campfire at night, and to keep the fire going. The girls had used some cloth and made him a straw mattress, so he could sleep under the wagon.

I could see that Susie and Ruby had themselves a "play-pretty". The girls found more for poor old Ray to do than chopping wood and getting the bonfire going when we made camp each night. They were taking turns going with Ray to pick berries, nuts, wild onions, and poke salad. Mary and I took it that Ray loved his job, or should I say the jobs on the wagon train. Ray and the girls were also keeping the whole wagon train supplied with fish and game.

I began to give the girls, as well as Mary and Ray, shooting lessons. I wasn't expecting any trouble, but it pays to be ready. Times were hard and we met some poor folks along the way. It seemed the further west we traveled, the worse it was. And the lot of us was not even out of the state of Louisiana, yet. I guess everyone in those days had his or her reasons for going out west. Most all the newspaper advertisements, fancy hand painted signs, and hand bills read the same: "Go west young man". Open space, free land to settle - a new world was in sight as we traveled westward.

It was Saturday evening when Mr. Arthur Gates gave orders to circle the wagons for the night. As always, the young girls and Ray Colter began to gather up firewood for the bonfire in our circle of wagons. One could hear the chopping of the ax in the forest, and the running of a clear stream close by. Mr. Gates had selected a perfect location to camp for the week end. Everyone on the wagon train had voted to reverence God on Sunday; and have a church service for those wanting to attend.

The stream was brimming with fish for catching, and the green grass was knee high for the horses to graze on all day Sunday. Well, Sunday did come, and as usual, a fine breakfast started the new day. I think we all needed a day of rest, and I'm sure the horses did also; we had pushed them pretty hard all week. The one thing in the back of everyone's mind was that winter was coming on. It was noised in our midst that to spend a winter in a covered wagon would be a total disaster.

Ray and I had arisen early and eased down to the clear creek. Within an hour he and I had mopped up with trout and bream. We were somewhat proud of ourselves. especially after we got 'em scaled and prepared for a Sunday fish fry. We were hoping everyone could enjoy themselves and pig out. It was after dinner, and everyone had eaten a bunch of fresh fish and hoe-cakes. The women were cleaning up, and the men were just sitting around talking. There were a few folk on the wagon train that didn't believe in working on Sunday. They even turned their noses up at Ray and me for catching all those fish for our Sunday dinner; but I noticed those same folk got in line to eat when the fish were fried.

What was the old saying - 'A squeaking wheel gets the grease'? Well! Arthur Gates, who had taken it upon himself to be ramrod of the wagon train, let it be known that a day of travel was no time to be hindered by someone having to stop and grease a squeaking wheel. Although it was Sunday evening, we all had chores to do and wanted to get an early start in the morning. The weather had been favorable for our travels so far, 'knock on wood'.

As I said, it was a lazy Sunday evening and the men were gathered in a huddle, planning their strategy for the upcoming week. Someone let it be known that a lone rider was coming into our camp. We had pulled the wagons in a tight circle; so it was impossible for anyone to get in.

"Hello there!" came a strange voice from outside our circle. Most every one turned around to see a middle-aged man sitting astride a horse, looking our way.

"I need to talk to the ramrod of this outfit." The men standing around all looked at Mr. Arthur Gates. as if to say, see what the stranger wants. Without any prodding, Arthur Gates turned and started toward the outside of our circle of wagons. I'm sure he had no idea if he was going to get shot or be given good news. I flipped the thong off the hammer of my trusting Colt, just in case there would be trouble. I, along with the rest of the men, followed Mr. Gates over to the stranger on the horse.

"I guess I'm the spokesperson for the group," Mr. Gates said, looking around at us, and propping his foot upon the tongue of a wagon. "Friend or foe?" he asked.

The man chuckled. "Well, it could be either one, depends how you take the news." By now we all stood spellbound.

"It 'pears you folks are heading west, and the route you are taking will carry you through the town of New Hope, probably about two o'clock tomorrow. Now, my advice to you is to by pass the town and don't stop for anything, not even an emergency."

The curiosity that killed the cat got to me, and I had to ask, "What seems to be the problem with the town, Mister?"

"As I was passing by, a man and woman, sitting on the side of the road, told me they were dying, and said that the town had a fever or plague, and everyone there was hungry, dead, or dying." I could see this news didn't set too well with two of the men of the wagon train.

"What do you suppose we do when we get there, Monday?" Mr. Clement asked.

"My suggestion to y'all is to hold a handkerchief to your nose and get through the town as fast as you can, and don't stop for anything!"

"But we are Christian folk, that's a hard pill for us to swallow."

"Since you folks are Christians, then we can share a little scripture with you. The Bible alludes to a lion being king of the beasts, but it also says: 'a live dog is worth more than a dead lion'."

"But, Sir, we consider ourselves to be good Samaritans," said one of the men.

"My good man, we are not talking about a beat up man lying beside the road, we are talking about a town that will die. Now you have been warned, I've got to be moving on." The man kicked his horse in the ribs and started off. Then, before we had time to discuss the issue, he whipped his mount around and came riding back. "You will see some dead bodies lying beside the road, near the town. I suggest you don't stop to bury the people; if it was me, I'd ride on by." Again the man whipped his horse around and left us standing there with a decision to make.

Of course, I had already made my decision about the whole ordeal. I was going to take the stranger's advice. But I knew I was going to have trouble with several of the men on the wagon train concerning this matter, because of their religion.

There wasn't much said as a group about the town up ahead, but I noticed the men talking among themselves to one and then the other. I knew that two of the men were headstrong and were following the leading of the Lord. But would the Lord have them go into a town where they knew for sure they would catch a fever that would kill them - and worse than that, bring it back to the wagon train and spread it to everyone around them?

I turned in before the rest of the troops on my wagon. Susie and Ruth were playing some fool game with Ray, and Mary was reading a book. Seems this is what she loved to do most, since she had learned to read. As Christmas is slow coming, but it does come, so did

Monday morning. Every man was busy about hitching up his wagon, and the women were cooking breakfast. Within the hour we were lined up and moving out.

One could almost tell it was a dread to get to the town where everyone was dying. The thought kept running through my mind, isn't there something we can do for these poor sick folks? I imagine everyone was pondering over this same question. I was hoping everyone on the wagon train would take the stranger's advice and pass this town and never give it another thought. Then the thought reversed itself. There were people in that town that were dying. What would they do for us if we were in their fix? Well, thank God, we will never know. Same as I, everyone had an eye out for the town we were nearing. The first indication of a town was a sign beside the road: New Hope - 5 miles. Strange as it may seem, these folks had no hope, according to the stranger that stopped by and warned us of the epidemic. Well, five more miles and we would know what was going to happen to the holy and religious bunch.

Mary had already warned Susie and Ruby to hold a cloth to their nose and sit quietly until we passed the town. I knew Mary had guts for this type of thing and wouldn't go off the deep end. I guess if you are around killing and dying, this hardens the conscience, and I think Mary had seen enough in her young life.

We had gone about five miles when the first or second wagon stopped right in the middle of New Hope. Of course, the wagon in front of me stopped to see why the others had stopped. Just what I thought. . .

I popped my horses across the rump with the reins and yelled as loud as I could... "Get up from here, horses, and you girls hold on back there," and away we went. As I passed Jessie and Julie Parks wagon that was right in front of me, I looked over his way and screamed out. "Follow me, man, don't you stop for nothing!" As I flew by Mr. and Mrs. Clement Dawkins's wagon I screamed out again, "Follow me, man, don't you stop for nothing!"

"Go ahead on, we will catch up later, me and the wife is going to help this couple!" he yelled back. The man and woman were lying right beside the main road going through town. When I looked back, he was getting down out of his wagon. By this time I was beside the Hicks' wagon. He was the other so-called preacher.

"Come on, Mr. Hicks, you are risking your life if you stop. Arthur Gates and Mrs. Mason were in the first wagon and saw me coming, and lit out. As they say, he wasn't letting any grass grow under his wagon.

I fell in line right behind the lead wagon, and the town of New Hope became a dot in the distance. Of course, we lost the Dawkins' wagon. It was already about four o'clock and I knew Arthur Gates was looking for a good place to camp for the night. I also knew we had a lot to discuss about the dead bodies layin' beside the road, and Mr. and Mrs. Clement Dawkins. What were we other members of the wagon train to do when he came back and wanted to join back up with the wagon train, and put us all in danger?

The setting sun was tipping the tops of the pines when I saw Arthur Gates turn off the road, and head down toward the edge of the tree line beside a small stream. A perfect spot I'd say; we had cover, and the horses had good grass to graze for the night. The girls had Ray perfectly trained; I saw him, with the ax and Susie, heading down in the woods. Ruby was not far behind. It wasn't long until we had a rip-roaring fire going. I was waiting for the topic of the day to be discussed. And I knew it was going to be a touchy subject. The Dawkins had lost Missy, their daughter, a week ago, and now we would have to turn them away from the wagon train. This was my vote, if it came to that. We were well into eating our supper when the subject was brought up about Mr. and Mrs. Dawkins stopping to help the man and woman laying beside the road.

"Has anyone given any thought to what we are going to do if Mr. and Mrs. Clement Dawkins come back and want to join our company?" Mr. Hicks asked, as he walked over closer to the bonfire.

"Are you asking for us to vote, or do you want a discussion?" asked Arthur Gates.

"I just want to know what everyone thinks about what he did by stopping to help these poor people."

"In my opinion, it was very foolish for him and his wife to stop and help. The stranger that stopped by warned us about the fever the whole town had," answered Jessie Parks.

"Well, it took all I could do not to do the same thing. But as you all well know, I am a preacher, and God has called me and my wife to go out west to preach the Gospel, not to die in the middle of Louisiana with some fever. That wouldn't be God's will."

"I think that was well put, Mr. Hicks, and I vote to turn Mr. and Mrs. Clement Dawkins away from the wagon train, should they come back, either tonight or tomorrow, and want to join up with us," stated

Arthur Gates. "We have young children to think about on this wagon train."

At least I now knew the thoughts of the people, and I didn't even need to give my two cents worth.

In all I had read and heard about heading west, this incident was just the tip of the iceberg. With only four wagons on the trail we were sitting ducks for robbers and outlaws to attack, easy pickings for hungry bandits and thieves along the way.

Chapter Thirteen

What was the old saying - "Don't change horses in the middle of the stream"? Well, we weren't gonna change horses...but we were going to change our strategy of how to face the future of this trip going west.

According to Arthur Gates the man with the map (such as it was), there was a rather big town up ahead called Pine Ridge. It had a well stocked general store. What we needed was powder and caps, and more guns. I had the money to buy anything that would shoot. The next challenge was to see each wagon armed with weapons, and to make sure every man, woman, and child could shoot a gun. If we were attacked by robbers ,they would be surprised.

I had already talked to the Parks from Bessemer, Alabama. Both he and his wife said if the wagon train was attacked they would have no trouble defending themselves.

"What if this means shooting a living soul dead?" I asked.

"The way I see it, Bill, it's either kill or be killed. When they take what they want from us, the criminals will leave no witnesses."

"Does your wife feel the same way?" I asked Jessie. He looked over at his wife Julie and she nodded. I thought to myself, Mr. Hicks will be the tough nut to crack when it comes to shooting guns, especially killing someone. After all, the Bible says 'Thou shalt not kill.'

"Just what does that mean Mr. Hicks, 'Thou shalt not kill?'" I asked. He also looked over at his wife, Angie, and she took him by the hand.

"What do you think it means, dear?" One could tell she had never been in a situation just like this before. She had lived a sheltered life before now.

"I know what the Bible says," she replied.

"But does the Bible change to fit our needs? Is this the time for killing, if we need to?" I asked.

"I know what you are saying Bill, self defense and murder are two different things…yet the person you kill, or just plain murder, because you don't like him…He's just as dead."

"But, will you answer my question; will you and your wife take up arms and help protect the wagon train if we are attacked?"

"Yes, we will, a person has a right to protect one's own self." I knew how Arthur Gates and Mrs. Mason felt about our rights, and knew that both of them would take the life of another, to protect their children.

I was being hard nosed I know, but I told everyone around the camp fire to listen up. "In case of an attack, we shoot to kill. Listen now, don't wait until you are shot at. Don't even listen to some sad story your enemy may try to tell you, shoot first and talk later."

Everyone here seemed to now know the seriousness of our situation. We were in a strange land plagued with road agents and outlaws. Thank goodness, we made it to the town of Pine Ridge the next day and camped just south of town. I was in luck, the town had a general store, hardware store, and gun shop.

Ray and I saddled both horses and rode into town, while the others set up camp. The hardware store was still open and had four Henry rifles for sale, and a dozen boxes of .44 caliber cartridges.

"We'll take them all, sir." I said to the clerk, and bought them all. The clerk was wide-eyed when I bought the nine pistols and all the black powder and caps he had in the store, plus a dozen or more holsters and gun belts. Of course, he was glad to get the money, and I didn't even ask the price. The General store was closed by the time Ray and I made our way over there.

"We can catch them in the morning," I said to Ray, and we went on back to camp, just as it was getting dark. Supper was ready. We all gathered around and ate before the guns were distributed. After supper all the woman worked together and cleaned up the dishes. Arthur Gates lit two oil lanterns; so we could see what I was about to show and tell everyone.

"Let's start with the ladies. Ray, if you would, give a pistol and a gun belt to each lady. Grace and Mrs. Hicks were somewhat hesitant at first, to take the gun rigging. But as they saw Susie, Ruby and Marge take the gun belts and try them on, they quickly complied.

"This may be fun," Angie said to Grace.

"Ladies, if the gun belt don't fit, make it fit; Mary has everything you may need in the wagon. Now, men, it is your time. Ray, give each of the men a new Henry rifle and two boxes of cartridges; give them a holster and gun belt, too. And the same goes for y'all, make it fit and make it comfortable; you will be wearing it day and night. That goes for you ladies also.

"Now, Arthur, if it's alright with you, let's stay here in camp tomorrow and you teach the ladies to load and shoot the pistols and rifles. Me and Ray will check out the General store for more guns and ammunition. I noticed the man over at the gun shop has a nearly new wagon and team for sale. If he hasn't sold it by tomorrow, I'm gonna buy it and let Ray drive it behind my wagon. I'm going to load it down with grain for the horses. I know, with healthy animals and guns, we well make it out west before the winter snows fall on us."

I might say, and being fair, the girls took to the six guns like a duck to water; I was just hoping they wouldn't shoot themselves in the foot. By the second day, every lady could draw and fan their Navy Colt as good as any man. I told Ray a man would be a damn fool to come against these ladies.

The next morning Ray and I bought three more Henry rifles and all the .44 cartridges in the general store and loaded the wagon down with grain, and salt. The ladies were out shooting cans and bottles. I walked up, with the three new Henrys tucked under my arm, to where the ladies were shooting their pistols. I gave Angie, that's Mr. Hicks wife, and Julie, a Henry.

"Where's my rifle?' Asked Grace. She was bent over setting up targets.

"It's right here under my arm, with two boxes of cartridges for you all. Now, if you get as good with these rifles as you are with those Navy Colts there isn't a desperado out west that will mess with us." As I walked away, they were feeding their Henrys. By the time I reached the wagon it sounded like a small war had erupted. That night at supper we sat around the bonfire and worked out a plan, just in case we were attacked by Indians, or bandits on the prowl.

"Do you have a plan, Arthur?" I asked.

"Well, it's for sure, we don't want the ladies to get hurt."

"I was thinking....at the first sign of any trouble, since you are in the lead. . .why don't you whip around meet Ray in the back wagon? Mr. Hicks, you and Angie in the second wagon, follow Arthur, and we will form a circle. If we happen to be by a river, we will form a half circle, and put our back to the river."

"Bill, you are always expecting trouble, why is that?" Angie asked.

"Well, it's simple, the Bible says the thief comes when we least expect him. So the way I see it, we must always expect the thief to come."

"One other thing I'm not sure about," Angie continued, "myself and the other women were talking this morning; when do we know to shoot and who to shoot at?"

"That's a good question, anytime someone threatens your life, or the life of anyone on this wagon train, either me or Arthur will shoot first; and that will be the signal for you ladies to shoot. Always shoot the person closest to you. That way everybody won't be shooting at the same person. What I'm saying is very important, this means life or death."

"Do you really think we will be attacked by thieves?" asked Julie.

"I don't know how many times I have to repeat myself, it's not what I think; it is just a matter of time before we will be hit. I know there are bands of men from the north and south that think the world owes them a living; and they are robbing and stealing from everyone, especially small wagon trains they can bully."

"The way you talk, Mr. Bill, scares us to death!" Ruby exclaimed, taking Mary by the hand.

"You listen now, ladies, the man that made that pistol you are wearing had a good saying, and I will repeat it in case you haven't heard; Mr. Sam Colt said, 'God made man, and I made man equal'. Now, Ruby, you need not be afraid of any big bad man; the pistol on your side makes you the same size as him."

Ruby reached down and patted her Navy Colt on her side. "I'm glad you told us that, Mr. Bill, now ladies, we need to practice more."

"That is right, ladies, as long as we are in transit heading west, handling a fire arm is just as important as baking good biscuits." I think the morale of the few people on our wagon was really lifted, when we turned in that Friday night. One thing about it, Ray had his own wagon now, and didn't need to sleep on the ground under our wagon. Ray had gotten pretty good with a six gun; his fast draw was above average and he could hit whatever he shot at.

It was Saturday morning and we got off to an early start. I guess the wagon train had gone several miles when a shot rang out (I took it to be from the front wagon). I reckon everyone's hearts jumped inside of them, not knowing what was going to happen next. I flipped the thong from the hammer of my Colt and put my hand on my Henry.

Ruby and Susie, having been out for a morning ride, trotted up beside my wagon, and Ruby asked, "You reckon what that was all about, Mr. Bill?"

"I don't know, why don't you and Susie ride off up that way and see who fired the shot." Mary and I sat and waited until we saw Ruby and Susie headed back. They were stopping at every wagon giving them the news.

"Mrs. Grace just shot her a nice six point deer all by herself!" Susie shouted, all excited.

"Well, ride back up there and tell Arthur to find us a good place to camp for the week end, we've been pushing pretty hard the last four days."

"Okay, Mr. Bill, they are loading the deer up, and Mr. Hicks is giving them a hand."

It wasn't but an hour until Arthur gave word to half circle the wagons on the bank of a river. Actually, it was one of the better places we had camped, plenty of grass, and everyone could take an all over bath.

The star attraction was Grace's two children, Jill and Garry, telling every one that Mommy shot a deer all by herself. Talk about a woman that was proud of herself! This gave the women encouragement that a woman could do more than just wash clothes and cook cornbread.

Ray and Arthur hung the deer on a low hanging tree limb and skinned it, while the ladies were waiting to start carving up steaks for dinner.

"Tell me now, Mrs. Grace, how did you kill that fine deer all by yourself?" I asked. There were several folk standing around listening.

"Well, Bill, there wasn't much to it after all. Me and Arthur were just riding along this morning enjoying the scenery, and breathing the fresh air. I looked to my right, and there stood a deer off about fifty yards or so. I told Arthur, 'I wish you would look...just standing there'. Arthur said, 'For crying out loud, Grace, shoot the deer; you got a gun laying in your lap.' Well, before a cat could think about licking her kitten, I pointed that new Henry right on the deer's front shoulder and squeezed the trigger. The rest is history; the deer went down, like you'd dropped a brick in a dug well."

"Now if you ain't something! By gum, we've been needing some fresh meat since we started this trip."

Oh well, in less time than it would take to tell it, we were enjoying fresh venison every way it could be prepared. I had me two steaks, from the young six point, that would melt in my mouth. I thought, this Saturday dinner that will not be forgotten soon, thanks to Mrs. Grace.

For a few minutes we were all full, and had put aside our differences, doctrine, and the danger that was always lurking close by. Ruby and Ray were sitting on the tongue of a wagon, talking about no telling what. Ruby quickly jumped up and turned to the group of men that were sipping coffee and talkin'.

"There are riders coming!" she yelled out. I ran to where Ruby and Ray were stretching their necks looking. My observation from a distance was that it could be ten or twelve riders coming. They weren't on the main road, but coming along the river bank, all spread out.

I turned to the ladies and men and yelled out, "Get a rifle and spread out behind a wagon, this don't look good!"

By the time the mangy looking bunch rode up, I counted eleven of the worst looking thugs I had ever seen. It was plain to see they weren't here to share the Gospel with us. The leader rode forward and pulled up his horse. The other ten men were lined up like purple martins on a telegraph wire. As far as I could tell, they were each packing a six-gun and holding a repeating rifle. Ray and Ruby stepped behind the wagon and left me standing alone, between two wagons.

"Are you the ramrod of this outfit?" the man out in front questioned, as he turned his head and spit out a mouth full of tobacco juice.

I took a step toward the man. I had already flipped the thong off my trusty Navy Colt, and dug my boots into the soft sandy river bank soil. "I might be. Who wants to know?"

The man turned his head both ways and looked at his mob of cut throats. "The boy wants to know who we are!" They all started laughing. "I can't believe you haven't heard of the Benson Gang, out of Arkansas; why we are more feared than the James Brothers and the Dalton gang put together." He spit again and took off his hat, and with his sleeve wiped the sweat from his forehead. "Now I tell you what I'm gonna do...have your men come, stand behind you, and throw their guns on the ground so we can see them."

"What about the women folk, what do you want them to do with their guns?"

The men all started laughing. He spit again and looked both ways. "The boy wants to know what we want the woman folk to do....are we gonna show 'em, or not?" I had an idea this pissed the ladies off real good.

"We gonna take one of your wagons, and we gonna load it down with food stuff, and we probably won't hurt anyone if y'all will do what we say."

That was the last straw. "You are a baldfaced liar, and you have met up with the wrong bunch." I drew my pistol and fanned three shots in his direction before he touched the butt of his pistol. Well, I'm here to tell you, within the next few seconds, it sounded like a small war. There were eleven men lying on the ground, and two horses shot full of holes. One poor fellow was shot off his horse. He started crawling off, and was shot seven more times, as I counted the shots.

Chapter Fourteen

All I can say is...at a time like this...we had a mess on our hands, and didn't quite know how to handle it. It seemed everyone was looking to everyone else for answers. And it appeared that they were looking to me, just a nineteen year old boy, to come up with the answer. It was as if they were thinking - it was your idea to teach everyone how to shoot a gun. Could you permit me to say: 'What happened when the dog caught the wagon wheel? He found out he couldn't drive the wagon'.

Within minutes, everyone in the camp was standing over the dead men, with smoking Colts and Henry rifles.

"Ray, you and Susie catch up the horses, get Ruby to help you," I encouraged. Then pointing, I directed, "Tie them up over there so they can't run off." By this time, Arthur and Mr. Hicks had eased up beside me, more or less looking for instructions.

"Don't you think we need to get the saddles off the two dead horses, so we can drag them away from camp?" Mr. Hicks asked, getting my attention.

"Well, right now, these eleven dead men are more important, don't you think?" Mr. Hicks looked at me with a blank look. I stood there trying to make a decision, one way or the other. I was thinking that Jessie Parks might have had the best idea.

"Why don't we unload the feed out of Ray's wagon and haul the whole dead bunch back to town? Didn't they have a sheriff?" As the four of us stood by the corpses, pondering the unsightly scene, a covered buck-board drove up. I guess the thought came to us all; was this more trouble, or just a passer by? I can say one thing; it didn't take long for a man to unload his lanky frame from the buck-board. He came walking through the pile of dead bodies, toward us. We just stood there. The ladies had formed a huddle next to the wagons, debating on who shot who.

"Let me introduce myself, I'm Larry Morris, a newspaper man from Little Rock. I've been following the Benson gang for the last five months. I'm also writing a book, and it looks like you people might have finished the last chapter, or started a sequel to the one I'm finishing on the Benson Gang."

"My name is Bill Allen, and this is Arthur Gates; he is the ramrod of this wagon train."

"I certainly want to get comments from each of you. If you only knew how dangerous this gang was; and you killed them all. Why the reward is enormous for what they are worth, dead or alive." The lot of us just stood there somewhat dumbfounded. We all marveled at the news this man in the derby hat and black suit was sharing with us. "Now if you men will be as kind as to help me prop up the gang, I want to take pictures before rigormortis sets in. And if you don't mind, I would like to have the wagons in the background. I would prefer to have all of the shooters standing behind the dead bodies."

"I think that can be arranged, just tell us what you want from us," Arthur Gates told the newspaper man. The ladies had gotten word of the reward; and each picked out the man they had shot, leaving us men completely out.

"As soft as this ground is, why don't you men get a heavy stick for each man. Drive the sticks in the ground, and we'll prop and tie the men to them. Be sure you lay their rifles across their laps, and make sure I can see their faces...I'll be setting up the camera, which is in my wagon, while you men set up the bodies."

While we were dragging the men around in front of the wagons, and propping them up, the ladies were making sure there every hair was in place, for the camera picture. The ladies had decided to stand behind the man they had shot, and this was causing some confusion. From left to right on the front row, were Angie, Julie, Mary, Ruby, Grace and Susie. Behind the women stood me, Jessie, Arthur, Ray and Mr. Hicks.

By now Mr. Larry Morris had the camera equipment set up, and took our picture from several different angles. The women went back inside the circle of wagons.

"Since you have the pictures, and you can be a witness that all the Benson Gang are dead, we can go ahead and bury the buzzards, don't you think?" I asked Larry Morris, the newspaper man. He thought it was a good idea. We had three or four shovels on the wagon train and every man volunteered to dig. I showed the men where to start digging: and told them Ray and I would bring the men to them, one at a time. They went to the spot and started digging.

"Now, Ray, hand me that wash tub hanging on the side of that wagon." I guess Ray was wondering what I was going to do with the wash tub. "Let's strip the men clean, except for their shirts, pants and boots. Throw what they have in the tub." The first man had over six hundred dollars in his pocket. As Ray and I frisked the men, he and I drug their bodies down to where the men were digging holes. Each body had a bunch of money on it, some more, some a little less; we kept all the pistols, gun belts, and rifles.

It was near dark by the time we finished planting all the outlaws. Susie and Ruby had a big bonfire going, and the other ladies had started frying up deer steaks again, for supper. Ray and I put the wash tub, along with all the saddles and whatever else they were carrying, such as watches rings and knives, into his wagon. Arthur and Jessie hooked up a team and drug the two dead horses a half mile from camp. Tomorrow would be Sunday, and we could rest all day.

Larry Morris asked Arthur Gates if he could tag along with the wagon train and write about our trials and tribulations along the way on our trip out west.

"What do you think about this endeavor?" Arthur asked me.

"Hey, my good man, the more the merrier, I hope he's not a big eater." We both got a big laugh.

"He said he would pay his way, and make his presence worth while." We also found out that Larry Morris was quite religious and from a very religious family. He said his father was a circuit rider and was wanting to come west in the near future.

It was Sunday morning and everyone was up and about. I'm sure Mr. Hicks had us a good hot sermon from hell ready for our morning message. After we had killed all those folks yesterday, I'm sure he was not without a Bible scripture to preach from..

After Ray made sure the fire was going, and the ladies were cooking breakfast, he eased over to where I was checking a wheel on my wagon, and squatted beside me. "I took the liberty, before I turned in last night, to count all the money in the wash tub. Would you like to make a guess how much it was?" Ray asked, smiling all over himself.

"I have no earthly idea. I know the first man we searched had over six hundred dollars on him."

"Bill," he said, appearing almost startled, "there was over three thousand dollars all total; and that was just in paper money alone. Now don't you think that's too much money to be laying around in my wagon?" I put the grease bucket down, and we both stood up.

"Now, Ray, I take you for an honest man. And I have no reason to doubt you ever. Let this be a secret between you and me. If you will, count out two hundred dollars to put in your pocket, and bring me the remainder." I took Ray by the arm and looked all around. "I have a safe place to keep the money until we get out west." Ray never questioned me, but nodded and started toward his wagon, where the wash tub and all the saddles were.

No one knew....not even Mary knew about the false bottom in the box where I had all the money from the houseboat and also, the money from the two bank robbers I had killed, when they tried to steal my horse. That was many moons ago, as the ol' Indian would say. Now, I needed to answer the one question that Mary had asked me several times. 'Since the west is a big country. where are we going?' I guess what they all wanted to know was where we were going to settle down. That would have to be up to everyone else. These were the thoughts going through my mind - Mr. Hicks is a preacher and he and his wife need to settle in a town that needs spiritual help. Then there is Jessie and Julie, they need a place to raise that baby they are going to have. I watch Susie and Ruby as they play up to Ray; he'll make up his mind one day and choose one or the other. 'Course there is Arthur and Grace, with Jill and Garry to make a home for.

I hung the grease bucket back in its place and started to walk over to where breakfast was being served. As I took a step around the wagon, there was Ray with a flower sack tied at the top.

"Here is the money, Bill." I took the sack and thanked Ray, then started climbing in the back of my wagon. Ray turned and started to where breakfast was being served. I went ahead and removed the false bottom and placed the sack with the other money inside. I replaced the false bottom and stacked the other contents on top.

It seemed that everyone on the wagon train referred the newspaper man to me. Rather than answering his questions, they suggested I would know more about what was going on. Well, that might have been true, in a way. I know one thing he was a very inquisitive individual, to say the least. He thought what the ladies did to the Benson Gang was historic. It would make news back east and sell many papers, especially with all his gory pictures of eleven dead men.

Larry Morris gave me the grand tour of his small covered wagon. It was set up like a photography shop; he explained how he had everything one needed to develop negative and make eight by ten prints he could ship back east to his office. He and I talked for the longest, and I suggested several times that he not make me a hero. I didn't want to get my mug in the headlines. I told him all I knew about everyone on the wagon train, without digging up skeletons and their personal lives. I did mention the preacher that raped Missy, and how Mr. Clement Dawkins shot him dead. Then Dawkins' mentally disturbed daughter drowned herself in the big Mississippi while we camped nearby on the bank of the river. The day after, he and his wife pulled out of the wagon train to stop to help a dying town, and we hadn't seen hair nor hide of them or their wagon since.

I was kinda dreading the river crossing Monday morning we had the wagon cracks corked with cotton and tarred, to keep them dry and floating. This would be the first river we had had to ford, since we started our trip out west. This was the shallowest place on the river, and I presumed this was why we had chosen to cross right here. I wouldn't want to cross if the river was up, and it looked like the whole bottom was going to fall out of the sky any minute. As a matter of fact, it had started sprinkling before the last wagon came across. I pulled to one side to make sure everyone made it safely across, include Larry Morris, the newspaper man.

All in all, we had no trouble. Some of the horses were spooked at first, but stayed in line and went on across. I was hoping Arthur would soon find a good place to pull up and weather this storm. I knew it was still early but the wind and blinding rain was becoming a hazard to each driver. We were about a mile from the main body of water when Arthur pulled his wagon up beside a tree line for some cover from the blowing rain. The others followed suit. and the rain seemed to get worse after we circled the wagons.

After a three hour downpour, I just figured it had set in for the night. There was no way one could get out in this storm, even to fix supper. We had not unhitched the horses from the wagons yet, and thank goodness. Although we were a mile from the river, we were in the river bottom, and the river was rising fast.

"Bill! Bill Allen, are you in there?" I could barely hear a voice calling over the wind and heavy rain, beating on the canvas covering on our wagon. "Bill Allen!" There it went again, I quickly removed a strap off the bottom flap and stuck my head out. There stood Larry Morris. "What do you want, man?"

"We've got to move the wagons fast, Bill, the river is rising; the water is near up to my axles."

"Did you tell Ray yet?" I yelled.

"No, he must be asleep!" Larry yelled back

"Well, wake him up, and you two take in behind me. I'm going to higher ground." When I went by Jessie Parks' wagon I yelled out as loud as I could, "We've got to get out of this river bottom or we're gonna be flooded out!" I did the same with the Hicks wagon and Arthur Gates. There was enough lightning flashing so I could halfway tell where the road was. I have no idea how far I went, but I felt I was on an incline, and thought this place would be as good as any. I had an idea no one would be out in this type of weather anyway. It had slacked up enough to unhitch the horses and corral them up for the night.

I had hoped everyone might have gotten enough sleep; the storm blew on over about two hours past midnight, and things calmed down. It was a beautiful sun shiny morning, the birds were singing, but it was going to be some muddy travel until the road could dry out. Arthur managed to get the wagons back in line, while the ladies prepared breakfast. Lucky for Ray, he had some dry fat lighter kindling in his wagon for emergency use. And if this wasn't an emergency, I don't know what was. We had all missed supper last night because of the rain. We knew it would be a slow day for our travel because of the muddy road and overflowing streams.

The wagon train was still drying out. We had gone about a mile when Arthur sent word back by Ruby, who was riding Mary's horse and calling herself a scout for the wagon train.

"Mr. Arthur said to tell you there were two covered wagons a ways up the road, and to him they look as if they are stopped. He is going to pull up and stop until maybe you and Ray can go up and check the situation out; it may be a trick, and others may be hiding in the bushes."

"Well, go back and loan Ray your horse, and I'll take mine from Susie, and he and I will ride off up there and check the wagons out." As Ray and I passed by Arthur's wagon we found he had already stopped.

"Just keep your Henry ready, you and Mrs. Grace. It ain't no telling what we are up against now."

Arthur was right. As I approached the two wagons, it was plain to see the back wagon had big trouble. At the back of the wagon was an old man with a full beard, white as snow, dressed om overalls and a straw hat.

Chapter Fifteen

"Howdy do, Mister," I said as I rode up. I could tell he was hard of hearing and he was somewhat surprised when he turned around. He took his corncob pipe out of his mouth and spit.

"You wouldn't happen to have an extra wheel in your back pocket, would you, sonny?" I looked over at Ray, we both laughed.

"No sir, but we got a spare back there in our wagon, you look like you're loaded pretty heavy. What are you transporting?"

"A dad-gum sawmill, and it's been more trouble than it's worth. Now look at this, a busted wheel!"

"Now I wouldn't say that, I been looking for a fellow with a saw mill I could hook up with; my bunch is going out west to start a new life for our selves." A smile came across the old man's face.

"My name is Jeremiah Duke, and in the wagon in front is my daughter, Maggie Lofton, with her two young boys. Sir, we not only have a busted wheel, but we have run low on food. It is more than I can take." He hung his head and started walking off, bogging down in mud up to his ankles.

"Go tell Arthur to bring the wagons on up, everything is alright." I said to Ray, as I dismounted. I walked on over to where the old man was standing, with his back toward me. "Mr. Jeremiah, this is your lucky day," I said. When he turned around I saw the face of a man, beaten down and stomped in the mud of life.

"Sonny, my luck ran out many miles back. I've come all the way from South Carolina, going to a new world I'll never see."

"Oh yes you will, Mr. Jeremiah. My name is Bill Allen, and I will see that you and your daughter will get to the new land." He started shaking his head. "You don't understand, sonny, I buried my wife of fifty two years back in Alabama, and I buried my daughter's husband in Mississippi. I don't have a penny to my name; my life's savings is gone, and if it wasn't for Maggie and my two grand sons, somebody would find my body in Louisiana."

I could tell these were proud people and would starve to death before they would beg. "Could I meet your daughter, Maggie, and your grandsons?" He started sloshing through the mud, and I followed.

"Maggie, somebody wants to see you." The curtain in the back of her wagon slowly opened, and I swear, with God is my witness, I stared death right in the face.

"Hello Maggie, your pa tells me you have two sons." She opened the curtain wider and up popped two heads. "I hear you boys are going out west." Both boys looked at their mother. I could tell now this family had lost all hope.

"Yes sir, that's where we had started."

"No ma'am, that's where you and the boys are going!" I stepped to one side and looked toward my wagon and motioned for Mary. She and the two girls were standing out by the wagon, stretching their necks looking up this way. I motioned with my hand for them to run on up this way. "Maggie, I want you to meet Mary, my wife-to-be, and Susie and Ruby; they will be your baby sitters for a spell. Mary will be your nurse, until you get better."

Susie and Ruby each took a boy and headed back to our wagon.

"Maggie, honey, are you able to walk?" Mary asked.

"Barely, I'm so weak," Maggie replied, leaning back against the side of the wagon.

"That's alright, honey, you stay right here. I'll be right back with some food for you."

I walked on around where Jeremiah was looking at his broken wheel. "You wouldn't be interested in selling your sawmill, would you?" I asked. By this time Ray was rolling up a new wheel to put on Jeremiah's wagon.

"Well, I might, if I could find anybody that would give me anything for it. I doubt anybody from here and on west would know how to run a saw mill."

"You are probably right, but I sure would like to learn."

"You say you might be interested?" The old man asked. "You see, I'm getting a mite old, and since I lost my son-in-law, I don't have much use for it now. He was gonna run it when we got settled out west."

"Well, I'm gonna run it for you now, that is, if it's okay with you." I saw Arthur coming our way, with something on his mind.

"Bill, what you think about making camp here until the road dries out? There is plenty of good grass for the horses."

"That suits me fine. I want you to meet Jeremiah, he has a saw mill in that wagon." Arthur and Jeremiah shook hands, and became the best of friends over the rest of the trip.

"Go ahead and tell the ladies to start dinner. Ray and I will get a fire going as soon as we get this wheel on the wagon, so we can get it out of the middle of the road." I think making camp was the best thing to do; because it looked like another cloud was coming up. At least we were high and dry, you might say.

Thank goodness, the rain held off until after and everyone had eaten their fill of dinner. Jeremiah told us he had a portable tent in his wagon that was easy to erect. He suggested the men could sit inside and jaw, until time to go to bed. Well, since his wagon was close by, getting the tent was no trouble for Ray and me. In less time than it would take to tell it, we had the tent up, and we were waiting on the rain. The lot of us moved our chairs and stools inside the tent, and finished sipping our coffee.

Larry Morris and Jeremiah pretty much took up the evening conversation telling about their travels - what they had done and seen. Of course, Larry Morris, being a newspaper man, had traveled all over, and had covered some gory sights. Then Mr. Jeremiah with his wisdom and knowledge and gray hair had about seen and done it all. What is that they say: 'Time flies when one is having fun'? Well, it had flown, and was getting late. The cloud had passed on over and we discussed whether to get an early start or give one more day for the ground to dry up.

According to Arthur's map, such as it was... there was a rather large town about twenty miles on up ahead. Larry Morris was in hopes he could telegraph the story of the killing of the Benson Gang, and mail the negatives of the pictures of the eleven dead men to his home office in Little Rock. The few of us still under the tent thought it was time to get our sleep, Arthur took the lantern with him, and we all went to our wagons for the night. I had no sooner gotten to my wagon than I saw Larry Morris coming my way toting a lantern. I waited.

"We got a thief in our camp," Larry said, with some disbelief in his voice.

"What?" I exclaimed.

"We must have a thief in our midst, my wagon has been ransacked." This was hard for me to believe; right off I couldn't think of anybody on this wagon train who would do such a thing. I thought, did someone slip out of the bushes while we were not looking? After all, it was dark, and Larry Morris' was the last wagon in line.

"Have you assessed what they may have taken?" I asked.

"The only thing that really stood out was the three 8x10 pictures of the Benson Gang were missing. Then I quickly looked for the plates I took out of the camera, and they were gone. This is when I ran over here."

"Well, this eliminates someone out of the bushes, or a passerby. They wouldn't have known of the pictures. Why would some one in this camp want the pictures in the first place, do you think?" I asked, getting really concerned. Could it have been Ruby or Susie? I know it wasn't Ray or Mary, I was thinking. "The only idea I've come up with in this short time is, that someone wants the pictures destroyed."

"You're saying someone in the picture don't want the pictures to reach the newspaper," Larry stated, with a puzzled look on his face.

"Do you think the plates and pictures may still be here in camp?" I asked.

"Are you suggesting we search every wagon in the camp, in the morning? Why, that would be most embarrassing, don't you think?" Larry asked.

I thought about that for a second, "I don't think that's such a wise suggestion." "You know what I think, Larry. It's getting late, let's not cry over spilled milk, but play the hand we are dealt."

"You are probably right, because I got an ace up my sleeve."

I really didn't know what Larry was referring to, as he turned and started back to his wagon. I thought as I stood there in the moon light, it will all come out in the wash in the morning.

By morning the water should be dried off the road considerably, and we all were hoping we could make a good run. Some were hoping we would make it to the town of Platt. Arthur had implied he thought it was a thriving town that had made out pretty well during the War Between the States.

After I entered my wagon and got my muddy boots off, and lay down beside Mary, she whispered... "What was that all about?"

"I was talking to Larry, the newspaper man. Someone in this camp went into his wagon and took the pictures of the Benson Gang that he had taken of all of us." I was very close to Mary as I whispered in her ear. The only thing between us and Susie and Ruby in the back, was an old wool blanket strung up between us.

"Did you miss me today?" Mary lovingly asked, "I'll be so glad when you and I can get alone again, won't you?"

"Baby, truer words were never spoken." As I lay there trying to get off to sleep, with Mary lightly kissing on my face, I began to ponder over in my mind who could have taken the pictures, and the first man I thought of was Mr. Hicks. Why Mr. Hicks, I asked myself? He is a preacher...So was Mr. Mason, and he raped Missy, a girl that couldn't even defend herself. Maybe Mr. Hicks didn't want to be associated with all that killing. His picture in all the papers might ruin his reputation as a religious man.

Mary finally dropped off to sleep, leaving me with my intense thinking. You know, what about Jessie and Julie Parks? Does anyone know anything about them, other than that they are from Bessemer Alabama, and Julie is five months with child? I lay there thinking, what about Arthur Gates and Grace Mason? Surely they don't have a dog in this fight. I guess I went on to sleep thinking about Larry Morris, was he really robbed, or lying through his teeth about the whole thing?

We started our journey early the next morning, and everything went well. I let Jeremiah and his daughter, Maggie, in front of my wagon so I could keep a good eye on that sawmill, not supposing someone would swipe it out of his wagon. Mary informed me that Maggie was mending just fine. Mary said Maggie shared with her they were running out of food, and she did without eating, so the boys would not go hungry until they got some help.

We were now traveling with the nine extra horses that had belonged to the Benson Gang, plus mine and Mary's horses. Susie and Ruby had laid claim to two of the cream of the crop for themselves to ride.

"Hey, ladies!" I yelled out, "If you two have nothing more to do than ride up and down the wagon train looking pretty this morning, you have my permission to put them Henry rifles to some good use."

Ruby and Susie rode over closer to where I was holding the reins, pushing my team along the still wet road.

"What were you saying, Mr. Bill?" Susie asked, sitting proud in the saddle

"I said, why don't you and Ruby put them new Henry rifles to some good use this morning? If y'all will, ride on up ahead and knock us down a deer or a hog for dinner; seems the noise of the wagon train coming keeps them all scared back in the woods." I didn't need to say more. The girls popped their spurs across the ribs of their mounts and were gone. I had warned the girls earlier about getting away from the wagon where I couldn't keep an eye on them, but now since they had learned which end of the barrel of a gun the bullet comes out of, I gave them more liberty.

I reckon it might have been crowding an hour or so, and I hadn't seen hair nor hide of Susie or Ruby. Just before worry set in, I heard a rifle shot ring out; the echo rumbled through the forest.

"They must have shot something," Mary said. She was sitting across from me on the driver's seat, reading a book. Mary and I kept rolling along, waiting to get up to where Susie and Ruby sat beside the road waiting. with a hog tied to the end of a lariat.

"Well I see we are going to have fresh pork chops for dinner today, and ham for supper." Now you talk about two proud ladies!

"I saw the hog first, Mr. Bill, but Ruby shot him, she was a lot closer."

"Well you both did a fine job, and I know the whole wagon train will be proud of you for providing the fresh meat. Help Ray load your trophy in the back of his wagon, and tell him I said to make sure he bleeds and guts the hog."

After Arthur halted the wagons for dinner, Jeremiah told Ray that before he became a sawmill man, he was a mule skinner, and he would give him some lessons on how to skin a wild shoat. Mr. and Mrs. Hicks were de-boning and salting the shoulders and hams so they could be smoked.

Arthur was ready with his meat saw, and raring to saw up the pork chops. Grace and Maggie were standing by ready and a waiting with a frying pan, while the girls were getting the fire going. I would say within the hour I was gnawing on a cat head biscuit, with a golden fried pork chop between. I believe a hot meal and coffee, and few hours of rest for the horses never fails to cheer up a tired crowd. Larry Morris sat down where I was eating my dinner and began talkin' with me.

"Bill, if we don't make it to the town of Platt by the time we camp tonight, I want to borrow a horse to ride into town, if you don't mind. You know that ace I had up my sleeve?" Larry stopped talking and slyly looked all around. "Whoever vandalized my wagon and stole the plates and pictures of the Benson Gang didn't get the negatives. I was smart; I had already put them in a saddle bag along with the story, to take into town when I went."

"So the pictures will be printed in the newspapers after all?" I asked. "Do you think this will flush out the persons that robbed your wagon?"

"I believe so, I think now there is more to the pictures than meets the eye. But I can't put my finger on the intent of the person or persons who wanted to destroy the pictures. But I am sure they didn't want to ever see their picture on the front page of a newspaper."

Chapter Sixteen

Arthur found an ideal place to make camp about two miles from the town of Platt. There was a nice clear stream with plenty of high green grass. We could water all the horses and let them graze, as well. We also needed to fill the barrels on all the wagons and start supper. I was thinking I might ease off down stream and try my good smelling soap bar. I know it wouldn't hurt anyone's feelings. Second thought, I'd bet you a wooden nickel to a good day's work if I'd ask Mary, she would go with me. It was still daylight when Larry Morris saddled a horse and started to town. Mary and I, along with some clean clothes and my bar of good smelling soap, started down stream.

"Mary, darling, I need to ask you something...or maybe I should tell you something first." Mary had pulled off her clothes and was wading out in the stream, which I guess I was about waist deep. She stopped real quickly and turned toward me.

"Don't tell me you've seen a alligator!" By now I had stripped my clothes off, and was heading out to where she was carrying my bar of good smelling soap. I started laughing.

"Bill Allen! If you try something funny I'm gonna scream!" she said excitedly.

"Do you remember when we first met? You cooked rabbits and took a bath behind the wood stove in an ol' wash tub."

"I sure do, and then you took a bath...you want to know something? I was peeping when you pulled off your pants."

"Mary Brooks, you should be ashamed of yourself."

"Well I wasn't, Bill Allen! I wanted to see what I was getting,"

Mary said, putting her arms around my neck, and her nude, warm body up against me.

"How did you know you were going to get me, what if I had finished eating and just got on my horse and rode off?"

Mary squeezed me even tighter, letting her cheek rub mine. "I don't know, I really don't know, Darling, I try not to even think of what would have happened. I was so lonely there in that house all by myself...scared too, most of the time."

"What I wanted to tell you. . .and just don't say anything about what I'm going to tell you now, not even to Susie or Ruby, but the other night when all us men was under Jeremiah's tent, and all you women were in the wagons...someone went into Larry Morris' wagon and took his pictures of the Benson Gang. Did you see anything suspicious, as you know of?"

Mary let me have some slack, and then looked me right in the face. "No, but there is something else suspicious, as you call it; the girls have been noticing it ever since the team from Bessemer, Alabama joined the wagon train."

"You mean Jessie and Julie Parks? What's wrong with them?"

"For one thing, me, Susie, and Ruby don't think she is with child; certainly not five or six months pregnant. And besides that, we've been talking between ourselves; we don't even think they are married."

"You mean gossiping, don't you?" I knew this would get a response.

"Call it what you want to, Bill Allen, we aren't married either."

"I know, Mary darling, but we ain't running around telling everybody we are."

"Are you ready to go? I'm shriveling up," Mary said, pulling on me to get out of the water.

"Have you...or the girls...seen something that gives y'all a reason to be suspicious of Jessie and Julie?"

"No, not really, just a woman's gut feeling."

"You mean a woman's intuition," I added.

"If you say so, I don't even know what that means; just remember I only learned to read since you and I started on this trip out west."

"Like I said, let's just keep this robbery thing under our hats until we see what pans out."

It was late when Larry Morris returned from town and came by my wagon. I was sitting outside looking at the stars and listening to the crickets.

"I got the negatives mailed. I also sent a telegram to my paper telling them to print the story of how a bunch of women, on a westward bound wagon train, killed the whole Benson Gang ."

"I'll bet that news headline will sell papers across the east."

Larry Morris went to laughing, as he walked over by the fire and poured himself a cup of coffee. "You are probably right, especially when the James Gang reads how the Benson bunch of cutthroats were killed by a half dozen ladies."

"You still have no idea who may have gone into your wagon and stolen the plates and pictures of the Benson Gang?"

"No, Bill, I have racked my brain ever since it happened, and I haven't a clue. Of course, now, you have been on this wagon train since the beginning; you should have some idea who it might be."

"I was talking with Mary just today; she and the other girls think it may be Jessie and Julie, in the wagon from Bessemer."

"What would give them that idea, you reckon?" Larry Morris asked.

"I don't know, I asked the same question," I said, getting up. I was hoping my getting up would give Larry Morris the idea I was ready to go to bed. I guess he got the hint and he stood up and stretched himself.

"I think I might as well turn in, myself, Bill, I'll see you in the morning." With that said, he started toward his wagon. I looked all around makin' sure the camp was secure. Then I eased up into my sleeping quarters.

I usually do lots of thinking when I first lay down at night. Mary was already asleep, and so were the girls in the back. I think everyone had had a hard day one way or the other, chopping wood, getting water, building fires, cooking, and washing up dishes. 'Course, just sitting on a bumpy wagon seat is a day's work, if you ask me. I had no more than pulled off my boots and gun rigging, when I heard the drops of rain start pounding on the canvas cover of our wagon. Then, naturally, the wind picked up. Something told me right then, we were in for a rainy night. Like Arthur said: During dog days, one can never predict the weather'.

Soon morning came, but no sun light; it was still raining cats and dogs, as they say. Arthur thought it was a good idea to not even move the wagons today; although we were in a hurry to get to where we were going before winter. They say the snow starts early out west.

Me, being from south of Atlanta, Georgia, never saw much snow. Mary had seldom seen snow in central Alabama. She had drawn the curtain between us an' the girls. They were all in the back, practicing their reading.

"While you ladies are having school today, I think I'm gonna see if Ray wants to go hunting. I thought maybe he or I could knock down a deer, or maybe a bear." The rain had slacked off for a few minutes, so I saddled my horse and walked over to Ray's wagon. I knocked on the side of his wagon several times to get his attention; I knew he wouldn't be asleep, and was probably cleaning his guns.

"You want to go hunting? I don't think Arthur wants the wagons to roll this morning."

"Yes! Let me get my rain coat on." We both had the best of rain gear; it was like sitting under a tent. We hadn't gone more than a mile or so from camp and had seen nothing but mud holes and more rain. The rain had really picked up now.

I rode over close to Ray and remarked, "I believe the animals had more sense than we did, they all must be under cover."

"I know what you mean. Going hunting in the rain ain't the smartest thing we ever did." By now it was raining in sheets; Ray and I could hardly see where we were going.

"Ha! Bill, that looks like an ol' mine shaft over in the distance; if we're lucky there may be something to get under and wait out this storm." Sure enough, there were several dilapidated old buildings. The primitive mine was grown up with grass and weeds, but still had an opening. We rode in and dismounted; at least we were out of the heavy gusts of wind and rain.

"I hope it hasn't set in for the day like this," I said, looking all around.

"There is no way it can rain this hard all day, or it will flood the county!" Ray exclaimed, pouring the water out of the brim of his hat.

"If we can find a dry match, I think I'll start a fire," I suggested.

"Well don't let that stop you. I keep my matches in a can with a tight lid. You want some coffee?"

"Don't tell me you have coffee in your saddle bag," I remarked.

"Yeah, and I also have a coffee pot; it's not very big, but it will make three or four cups. I don't have but one cup with me, you can drink out of the pot."

Water and wood wasn't a problem; I found plenty of powder dry wood a few yards back in the old mine shaft. Ray located a stream of water, as big as your arm, running out of the rocks.

As the ol' fellow said: We had killed two birds with one stone. As we enjoyed a cup of coffee, we dried our boots at the same time.

"Bill, I believe the rain is letting up, what do you think?"

"It's about time, this smoke going everywhere is disturbing these leather winged bats, and I shore don't want to get bit by one of these ugly little varmints." I remembered what Mary had told me about her dog.

"Well, since it's stopped raining, maybe the animals have come out to graze. We need to keep a close eye out," said Ray, putting his rain coat back on. He and I mounted up and started away from the mine. I looked up at the sky, trying to make a decision on the weather.

"I believe you're right, did you see that? I believe it was a white tail deer."

"You might need to take another look, Bill ol' boy; it looks like a person, from where I'm sitting."

"Well, what in tarnation would somebody be running through these woods in this rain for?"

"I don't know, but let's find out."

Ray and I kicked our horses and took off after the figure in question, to see if we could help. We finally had to dismount to run after the person because the underbrush was so thick.

"Ray, you stay with the horses! I'll try to see what this man is running from, or running to." By this time I could only get a glimpse of a figure darting through the heavy vines and thicket. "Hold up a minute!" I shouted.

"No, no, get away!" cried a fear and tear-filled voice, which sounded like a female voice.

"Let me help you!" I shouted again. I was catching up with whoever it was. The brambles and thorny vines hanging from the trees were tearing into my flesh. When I finally caught up with the woman, she was tangled in the briars and brambles, and could go no farther. When I reached her, she fell to the ground, out of breath. Her clothes were torn to shreds and her face and arms were a bloody mess.

"What is it, woman? For God's sake, let me help you!" I could tell now the young woman feared for her life, and was blinded by the blood running into her eyes. She began to try to crawl through the thick underbrush, but her half torn off kimono was was caught up in the thorns of the brambles. "It's all right, lady, I'm just here to help you, now calm down." She began to wipe her face to see who I was; it was like she thought I was someone else chasing her. I saw that she was calming down. "Here let me help you up." I extended my hand and she began to try to get up.

"Who is it?" Ray yelled.

"It's a woman, Ray, she is scared to death. We're coming your way." She and I wormed and wiggled our way back through the thicket to the clearing where Ray waited with the horses.

"What is the problem with you, lady, an' could we ask who you are running from?" She was looking down at herself, trying to fix her clothes, what few she still had on. "Ray, if you will, hand me one of the blankets we have in our bedroll, there behind the saddle. Maybe they ain't all wet. Put this around you, ma'am. Won't you tell us your name?"

"My name is Gloria McCurry, and my husband is going to kill me if he finds me," she said with very slurred and awkward words.

"Well, he ain't gonna kill you while me and Ray is here to protect you."

"You don't know my husband! He's a McCurry, and the whole bunch is meaner than snakes," she paused, wiping her nose, "he won't even ask questions, he'll shoot both of you if he sees me with y'all."

"Ma'am, I don't want to disappoint your husband. . .if and when we see him. Both Bill and me has got a Colt strapped to our leg, and I'm just dying to shoot it this mornin'."

"Look, Gloria, I believe that's what you said your name was...I've got a wagon train heading west, no more than a mile from here. Now to my way of thinkin'...why don't you let us take you over there? We have some ladies that will take care of you. I'm sure girls will give you some dry clothes and food."

"Mister, I don't want to put you out. I may need to just go back home and take my beating, and try to make a go of it, since I've thought about it." She pointed, "I don't live far from here."

"Well, load up behind me, this horse will go either direction. I'll take you home." Ray and I made our way out of the thick brush and hit the main road.

"That's our shack up there, where the smoke is coming out of the chimney. If I was y'all, I would let me off at the corner of the field."

"Just hang on, my dear lady, you've got my blanket, and I want it back. . .you just go in and get you some clothes on, then you can give me back my blanket. Will that work?" I started down the lane between the two fences. Two or three dogs ran out from under the front porch and started barking as we neared the slab- sided building. Before Gloria even dismounted, the front door swung open and a poor excuse for a man walked out on the front porch. He looked like he had never taken a bath or shaved. He was naked from the waist up, and a pair of suspenders was holding up his loose-fitting, dirty britches. My second observation was worse than the first; he was holding a half bottle of liquor in one hand, and a ten or twelve foot black-snake whip in the other.

Chapter Seventeen

"Woman, you get your sorry ass off that horse right now!" he shouted, putting the bottle to his lips and taking a slug. Gloria did as told and slid off the horse behind me, dropping the blanket when her feet hit the dirt.

"Now, you sorry bitch, I'm gonna teach you to not run off this time; you catch the top wire on the fence and don't you turn loose or around." He took another slug of his whiskey and walked out in the yard. He set the bottle on the top doorstep. Still holding to the handle of the whip, he let its coil fall to the ground. "I'll see if I can strip the rest of that kimono off of your sorry ass, woman," he scolded, as he turned himself to begin the whipping.

I thought to myself, am I going to sit right here and let this vindictive ol' bastard take the hide off this woman or not? It's really none of my business.

"Hold it one minute, mister; before you start your whipping, we need to do some talkin'!"

"Young fellow. . .you and your buddy need to get your ass off my land. This is not gonna be a pretty sight when I finish with this bitch. She's done had two miscarriages, and she has done gone and lost my baby this morning."

The woman dropped to her knees and screamed out unmercifully, "It is because you beat me with your fist last night you, drunken bastard, I hope you kill me this time!" I had heard all I wanted to hear. This is when Ray slid out of the saddle and came around in front of his horse, mad as I had ever seen him.

"You lay one stripe on that woman, you son-of-a-bitch, and I will cut you down like a rabid dog." I thought it was all over when the man dropped the whip and spit at Ray. He turned, picking up his bottle, and went back in the shack. I walked over to help the woman get up. With my back turned to the shack I had no idea what was going on. I heard a shot and spun around just in time to see the man inject another round in his Henry, and point it my way. I dropped to the ground and rolled, fanning three shots into the chest of the man, as he stood on the porch. The Henry rifle slipped from his hands to the floor; then he buckled at the knees and blood gushed from his mouth. I started getting up as he fell to the floor and rolled out in the yard.

I ran over to where Ray was lying and saw that he was shot bad, I sat him up and pulled him to my chest. He began to try to talk.

"Don't say anything, Ray; I'll get you to a doctor."

He shook his head several times, and uttered his last words, "You tell Ruby I love her." His head drooped and he never drew another breath.

I eased Ray's body back to the ground and walked over to where the woman was kneeling by the fence.

"Get up and go in the house, and get you some clothes on. . .you are going with me, unless you have some kin near by."

She shook her head and started getting up, "I don't have anyone. My husband has three brothers not far from here, and it would be worse living with them." I caught hold of her arm and helped her to the porch of the shack.

"Get you some clothes on, and pack what you want to carry with you. I'm going to borrow your buck-board settin' behind the house, and the horses in the corral."

Gloria stopped at the door and turned facing me with a look of disbelief and asked, "Why are you doing this?"

"Well, lady, it's the only thing to do right now, don't you think?"

"No one has ever done one good turn for me, and now you are gonna get yourself killed over it."

"Why do you say a thing like that?"

"I told you my husband was a McCurry; they stand together and they fight together. When they find out you killed their brother your life ain't worth a plug nickel."

"Well, you let me worry about that, now do what I told you. Your arms and legs need some doctoring. I'm carrying Ray's body back to the wagon train for a decent Christian burial." I was almost finished hitching up the wagon to the horses when Gloria came walking out the back door of the shack, toting a grip.

"Do your husband's have brothers live close by? Maybe we can carry the body over to their house. Just maybe the kin folks might have respect, and can bury him." I helped her on the wagon, and we took off, only stopping to get the two bodies and the man's Henry rifle.

"My husband and his three brothers make whiskey together up in the hills," Gloria pointed. My husband was the one that grew the corn for the sour mash."

"I still think we need to carry his body to his brothers."

"Well, you can do as you like, but you don't know this bunch of McCurrys like I do; there is no reasoning with them. All they know is fighting and killing."

"How did you ever get mixed up with this bunch of moonshiners in the first place?"

"Well, Sir, you ain't setting on this wagon seat with an angel yourself. But I've had the living hell beat out of me so many times I've seen the light. You should of let him kill me a while ago; I wished I had of took that bullet, instead of your friend laying back in the wagon."

"Well, what has happened has happened, and we must go on with life. I ain't blaming you or myself, but my friend, you call him, and he was. . .shouldn't have turned his back on that damn fool husband of yours, he done told us he was gonna kill the two us, just as soon as he got you whipped."

"You need to turn down that three track road right up yonder; it goes to Carl's house, that's his younger brother." She and I had only gone half mile or less when I spied a house in the distance, if one could call it that. There was a NO TRESPASSING sign nailed on a fence post beside the road.

"That's him out in the yard chopping wood, and from the looks of it he is wearing his pistol." He saw us coming and stopped chopping, then leaned up on the ax handle. I pulled the horses up within ten or twelve feet of the wood pile and stopped.

"Y'all didn't see the sign?" he asked as he let go of a mouth full of tobacco juice.

"We saw it, but I can't read," I answered. I had an attitude dragging when I drove up, but I think it was getting longer by the minute.

"Where is Doris?" Gloria asked. "Is she in the house?"

"No! She ain't in the house, she left about two weeks ago, went down to Jackson I heard. . .any how, she took the boy with her." He spat and took a step toward us. "I'm going after her when I get me a horse, and Bruce pays me next week. I'm thinking I may kill her. It's for sure I'm gonna bring the boy back, if he goes to kicking and screaming it's gonna be Katie bar the door, I'll wring his neck." Gloria and I just sat there on the wagon seat and let him ramble on. "By-gum, Gloria, ain't that Dykes' wagon you and that feller is riding around in? And that's his two horses; I know the brand. Does Dykes know that you are gallivanting around in his wagon?"

"Mister, if you will listen a minute I will tell you what happened to your brother, I think you called him Dykes. He was shot to death not more than an hour ago. I can tell you it was self-defense. He's back here in the wagon, along with the young man he killed in cold-blood."

Carl stuck his ax up in a block and walked over to the wagon. "I can tell you one thing, Mister, we McCurrys don't believe in self-defense. Whoever shot and killed ol' Dykes is gonna pay fer it."

As I jumped off the wagon I flipped the thong off the hammer of my trusty Colt, and walked around to where Carl was standing looking at his brother.

"I hope you understand, Carl, I was minding my own business this morning after the rain, and Gloria came running through the woods where Ray and I were hunting for deer. Well, anyhow I caught her and carried her back to her husband, Dykes. Now to make a long story short, he commenced to strip the hide off that woman sitting right there with a black snake whip. The young man, laying there beside your brother, sailed off his horse and stopped Dykes by drawing his pistol. Your brother dropped the whip and turned and went on in the house. Now I thought your brother had reconsidered and cooled down. I walked over to where Gloria was kneeling on the ground by the fence. I guess Ray holstered his pistol and was going to mount his horse, When your brother came to the door of the shack he shot Ray in the back. I heard the shot and quickly looked around, and your brother was about to shoot me."

"I told you, Mister, we McCurrys don't believe in self-defense.

"I tell you one thing you can believe in...If you go for that pistol hanging on your side, there will be two McCurrys laying over there on that front porch. Now, if you will be kind enough to help me unload your brother's body over there on the porch, I will be on my way." I watched him like a hawk; if I even thought he had the notion in his head to shoot me, I would have weighted him down with lead. If there was ever a man that needed killing, it was him.

I eased back over to the wagon, never turning my back on the buzzard. "Oh by the way, Carl, I have a wagon train about two miles, give or take, just east of town. You can come by tomorrow and pick up your brother's wagon and horses; I'll feed them good tonight." I got up in the wagon and drove off...knowin' full well I wasn't through with this bunch of McCurrys." I don't guess Gloria said a dozen words before we drove up at the wagon train. I knew the worst would be yet to come, when Susie and Ruby found out about Ray.

They had a bonfire roaring, and were about to start supper. I guess every eye was on me - sitting with a strange woman and Ray's horse tied behind the buckboard. Mary was the first to the wagon.

"Where is Ray?" she asked.

"He's dead; hold Susie and Ruby back, he's not covered up." Mary ran toward the girls, "Y'all don't go out to the wagon, Bill said."

Ruby fainted right there in her tracks, and Mary and Susie had all they could do to deal with her. Of course, by now everyone on the wagon train was gathered around the buckboard looking at Ray. I eased over to where Mr. Hicks was standing.

"I want you to say a few words over Ray. Do you think we ought to bury him today or wait until tomorrow."

"Bill, I suggest we take him on to town, we still have plenty of daylight, and let the mortician give him a proper funeral tomorrow. He needs to be buried in a graveyard with other folks, don't you think? I'll even ride with you."

I motioned for Mary and explained, "Me and Mr. Hicks is going to carry Ray's body into town to get him all fixed up; we can have his funeral tomorrow." It wasn't that far, and the town was closer than I thought it was. We had no trouble finding the funeral parlor and funeral director. Mr. Troy Black was his name.

"Mr. Black I want Ray Colter to have a Christian funeral in a church, if there is one in town. And if you have any authority can you have him buried where there is other folk? You will find at least two hundred dollars in his pocket; buy him a three-piece suit, and put a marble stone on his grave, and can you make it read 'I GAVE MY

ALL'?" Mr. Black immediately took charge, and said the body would be ready and prepared for burial at ten o'clock tomorrow, at the white church at the end of town

As Mr. Hick and I came near the wagon train, we could tell they had a rip-roaring bonfire going. And as far as I could tell, there wasn't a dry eye in the crowd. Gloria had told her story - how she had lost a baby and how her husband went to get a whip; how she ran out of the shack and kept on running. She told how bravely Ray gave his life to save her from a brutal beating. Ruby had finished the story of how she and Ray had fallen in love, and were planning to get married at our church service, in camp on Sunday morning, because she was carrying Ray's baby.

The ladies had saved me and Mr. Hicks some supper that was mighty good. Before the group started putting up the dishes and going to their wagon, I told them what we were up against with the McCurry brothers. 'Course Gloria had already warned the folk of the danger we would face, until we were gone, or they were all killed.

"But surely, Bill, this bunch will think the situation over and let it pass," Arthur remarked.

"I hope so, Arthur, but I have never seen or heard of a bunch as heartless and hateful as this bunch of buzzards. You ought to hear what Gloria told me on the way over here. Why, one of the brothers, Carl, is going down to Jackson next week - to kill his wife - and to get his little son back, to pollute his life with whiskey and a vulgar mouth."

I didn't know how many of our group would be going to Ray's funeral in the morning; we had a dozen horses and saddles for those who wanted to go.

"By the way Mary, what did you do with Gloria?"

"I gave Gloria Ray's wagon and bed, sad to say he won't be a needin' it anymore. Ruby said she would do the driving. She is going out west with us, isn't she?"

"Well, I guess so if she wants to, she said she doesn't have any place to go. Where was Jessie and Julie tonight?"

"They were over for supper, but done went back to their wagon before you and Mr. Hicks returned from town. You know something, Darling, they sure are acting strange, if you ask me!"

"Well, I didn't ask you, but I kinda know what you mean. In the morning, I want you girls to deck out with your Colts hanging low and tied to your legs; I just might need some help if that bunch of low-life McCurrys shows up."

"Are they as mean as you say they are?"

"Mary, honey, don't let this get out and spread through the camp, but that whole bunch needs a good killing."

"After Gloria got through telling Ruby what all happened to her while she was married to that scoundrel, Ruby said if she ever got the chance, she would kill the whole damn bunch right by herself."

"Well, I can understand her feeling; Ray Colter was a good, young man, near the same age as me."

Chapter Eighteen

It was Saturday morning. It was lightening and thundering in the west and looked as if we were going to get a down pour, just any minute.

"We can't wait on the rain this morning; never can tell, it may pass us by," Arthur explained, as he threw some wood on the smoldering coals from last night's fire. Angie and Grace had two Dutch-Ovens sitting in the coals, and Mrs. Hicks was putting her cast iron frying pan to good use. 'Course now, the weather looked so threatening that it deterred most of the camp from going to Ray's funeral. Mr. Hicks was obligated to go, since he was going to give the message at the funeral. That left me, Mary, Susie, and Ruby to chance the rain this morning.

It looked more like we were going to a Wild West rodeo than to a funeral. Mr. Hicks wore a black suit and tie. The girls were wearing their boots and tight britches, with a Navy Colt hanging low, tied to their leg; now, if they weren't a sight for sore eyes, I'll pay for lying. It seemed that the four of us kept expecting the McCurry brothers to show up shooting, any minute.

Thank goodness, we made it to the church without getting wet, it seemed as if the weather, and the Man upstairs, was favoring ol' Ray today. The funeral director had hired an organ player and six pallbearers, I can say one thing, ol' Ray was getting his two hundred dollars worth. When Ruby looked over in that casket she took it mighty hard. A good man now days was hard to find; twenty percent of the young men from the South to died in battle in the War Between the States.

As we stood and looked at Ray for the last time, lying there in his black suit and vest; he had a smile on his face. Maybe dying wasn't so bad after all. The four of us sat down across from the six pallbearers; we held hands while Mr. Hicks took his Bible and began to read: 'In my Father's house are many mansions, if it were not so I would have told you. And if I go and prepare a place for you, I will come again, and receive you unto myself…' I thought to myself, sitting there by the girls lined up on the front row of that little country church - that's a far cry from Ray sleeping in that covered wagon with all them sweaty saddle blankets and saddles. Mr. Hicks ended his sermon by saying: 'that where I am, there ye may be also.' The girls were all crying, especially Ruby. The funeral director walked up to the casket and motioned for the six pallbearers to come forward. Ruby really broke down when the lid was closed and the organ began to play. The funeral director motioned for us to rise and follow the casket to the cemetery behind the little, white church.

It was plain to see that Ray Colter had made his choice between Ruby and Susie; and I believe the two girls knew his choice. Susie was holding Ruby, trying her best to console her, as we neared the freshly dug pile of red clay. The six pallbearers carefully placed the coffin on two timbers that were across the top of the grave and stepped back until Mr. Hicks concluded the service. We could hear the organ playing in the distance.

Believe it or not, the sun was trying to come through the dark, low-hanging clouds. The girls had somewhat regained their composure as we turned and started back to our horses, tied up in front of the little, white church. As we slowly approached our horses, we knew that there was going to be trouble.

There sat Gloria's husband's buckboard, and two more horses tied to the back of it. We all knew the brothers had been by the wagon train and gotten the wagon, and found out that I was at the cemetery this morning. Lots of things began to run through my mind as I came closer. I motioned for the three girls to get behind me.

There was no denying who I was up against; there stood Carl in the row of scum. Gloria was right; the McCurrys were going to avenge their brother's death, even if they were wrong. I stopped about twenty feet from the three to make my play. I didn't know how fast the McCurry brother were, and they were all three wearing pistols hanging low. I flipped the thong off the hammer of my Colt. I had never been up against these odds; three against one was pushing it to the limit of a twenty year old, Georgia country boy.

"Is that him, Carl?" one of the brothers asked.

"That is him, Bruce; he was the one that was riding around with Dykes' woman and killed him."

Before anything else was said, Ruby stepped right in front of me...more or less just pushed me back. While I was trying to think straight, Mary stepped up on my right side and Susie on my left.

"I heard you McCurrys don't believe in self defense. Y'all killed my man, but he put a seed inside of me that you bunch of McCurrys will never be able to harm" Ruby scolded, and went for the Colt hanging on her side.

As far as I could see, none of the three brothers had even cleared leather when the three girls drew and started fanning their Navy Colts – creating a sound like a small war. I just looked on. I could tell Ruby had a gut full, and was mad as hell. She pumped two chunks of lead in the chest of Bruce McCurry, his knees began to buckle and he looked wild eyed, as the blood gushed out. He was falling to the ground and she fanned off two more shots in his whiskey-bloated belly; when he hit the ground she finished emptying her revolver with two last shots. I thought for a minute she was going to throw her pistol at his bleeding, dying body - piled up on the ground beside those of his two brothers who had been shot by Mary and Susie.

The three girls turned around and looked at me, just standing nonchalantly, sucking on a straw.

"Well!" Ruby said, blowing the smoke out of the barrel of her Colt.

"Well....join the crowd, young lady." By this time the undertaker had walked up and was looking at the three bodies.

"It sure doesn't take you ladies long to drum up business, does it?" They looked at me and shrugged their shoulders, as to say: All in a day's work at the office. They turned and went to their horses, and left me talking to the undertaker.

"Can you bury these men for me?" I asked, taking a wad of money out of my pocket.

He looked a little surprised. "Yes, but not in that cemetery," he turned and pointed to where we had just been.

"I don't give a rats butt where you plant them, I just don't want them lying here rotting, in the front yard of the church. I imagine they will have service here in the morning."

Mr. Hicks was standing near when this all took place, and didn't give his approval or disapproval one way or the other.

"Mr. Hicks, why don't you and the girls try to make it to the wagon train before the whole bottom falls out?" It had started sprinkling drops big as quarters. "I got this situation under control." Mr. Hicks and the girls made themselves scarce without any coaxing or persuading.

"As I was saying. I can't bury these moonshiners in that cemetery, but I do have a place not far from here where I bury heathens and outlaws; I'll give 'em a new pine box and a deep grave for twenty five dollars apiece." I thought, as I pulled off a hundred dollars out a roll of bills, that is a deal.

"Here is a hundred dollars, I'm taking their gun rigging and the horses and wagon. They may have some money on them," I said, pulling the holsters off the bodies. The rain had picked up considerably as I got on the wagon and started toward the wagon train. By the time I reached the camp I could barely see where I was heading.

Back at camp the rain had almost put the fire out and everyone was in the wagons trying to stay dry and warm. Mary fixed me a snack after I changed into some dry clothes, and she and I began to talk.

"Do you think the rain is set in for the night?" Mary asked.

"It sure looks that way," I answered.

"You have no idea when we are going to break camp and hit the road again, do you?"

"Your guess is as good as mine." And with those few words I reckon Mary and I went to sleep, listening to the rain and wind blow on the canvas covered wagon.

The next morning I was awakened by the sound of Arthur Gates voice calling to everyone on the wagon train, "Hitch up, we're moving out!" I think this was music to some ears.

It had quit raining sometimes during the night and most of the standing rainwater had either ran off or soaked in the dirt. We had about worn out our welcome in this spot; the horses had nibbled the grass down to the dirt and the girls had picked up all the fire wood close around the camp.

A bonfire was started and the smell of coffee was in the air. Everyone was stirring around like bees around a hive. Believe it or not, the sun was trying to break through this morning. I had talked it over with Arthur, and we were planning to put all the feed we were carrying for the horses in the buckboard, to give Gloria and Ruby more room in Ray's wagon. Although the road was wet and muddy, we were making good time. As the men on the wagon train had discussed time and time again - we needed to be where we were going before winter.

For the next week either dog days were over, or the good Lord was favoring us. According to Arthur's map, such as it was, he guaranteed us we would be in Texas by tomorrow, if the good weather held out. I think most on the wagon train assumed that when we crossed into Texas we would be 'out west'. We were shooting for Fort Worth and the land office. As I talked to others we agreed that we were seeing lots of open spaces and with nothing much of interest to look at. As Arthur had explained several times around the camp fire, this was the Wild, Wild West - not Alabama or Mississippi. I even think some were disappointed they had come west.

I was sure that many had traveled west for the same reason I did - to settle down and own a ranch with cows, as far as the eye could see. But others had the same idea before us. I never will forget, the first day we crossed over into Texas we had visitors - two men wearing three-piece suits, gold chains, and derby hats. Arthur had found us a beautiful place to camp for the night, plenty of water and grass for our horses. I was busy doing something when the two men rode into camp. Someone pointed out Arthur Gates, and told the two men he was Wagon Master. It wasn't long before I saw him and the two men coming my way. I stopped and waited for them.

"Bill, these men are Pinkerton Agents from back east" Arthur said, handing me a newspaper. "Do you recognize the picture on the front?" one of the agents asked.

"Yes, that's the Benson Gang, and all the ladies standing behind the bodies, why do you ask?" The two Pinkerton Agents looked at each other. "It appears that the woman that we have circled with a pencil is a fugitive from the law. We have been on her trail for the better part of a year. She is wanted for murder and bank robbery. She has used a number of names since we have been tracking her. As far as we know, she is heading to California and has in her possession over sixty thousand dollars she has stolen from northern banks - from Illinois to Tennessee. We noticed in the picture she calls herself

Julie Parks, and the man with her is Jessie Parks -- claiming to be her husband. It appears he is not wanted, but just along for the ride."

"We haven't had a minute's trouble with them since they joined the wagon train; they pretty much stay by themselves. But we know now why they ransacked Larry Morris' wagon, taking the plates and pictures," I explained to the Pinkerton Agents.

"They don't know who we are, or what we are doing here, and I doubt very seriously they will give up without a fight," the Pinkerton Agents said to me and Arthur.

"The way you talk, they are armed and dangerous," I said, looking toward their wagon.

"That is right, sir; you just don't know this woman and what we know about her."

"All I know is they said they was from Bessemer, Alabama and joined the wagon train in Vicksburg, Mississippi. We never minded their business and the same for them. They seemed nice enough to us, ain't that right, Arthur?"

"Bill is right, are you sure this is the right woman? According to what she has told some of the ladies on the wagon train she is five or six months with child." The Pinkerton Agents looked at each other. "That's her, that is Mae Bell Davis. We understand she has been using this story for years."

"That is right...not only is Mae Bell a bank robber and has killed several men, but she is a liar as well. She can tell a sob story that would bring a tear to a glass eye," the other Pinkerton Agent reiterated.

"If it is any of my business, how are you going to apprehend them? According to you, when they find out who you two men are they will make a run or start shooting. I just don't want anybody in my camp to get hit by a stray bullet!" exclaimed Arthur.

"Just wait one minute, this just may be some of our business. Didn't you say there's a reward for Mae Bell ? And isn't it so that a Pinkerton Agent can't claim the reward?" I asked.

"Just what did you have in mind?" one of the Pinkerton Agents asked, willing to listen to any idea to keep him from getting shot. "

According to Arthur, we will be pulling into the town of Sage, Texas about dinner tomorrow. I will give you Mae Bell and her boyfriend on a silver platter, without a shot fired. I will need two pair of hand-cuffs," the two Pinkerton Agents looked at each other.

"I'm willing, what will another day make, anyhow? It just might keep someone from getting shot or killed. Okay, we will be in the saloon waiting for you, and you will receive the reward on the two." With that oral agreement and a handshake, the two Pinkerton Agents rode off without another word.

"Now just how do you plan to apprehend the two of them?" Arthur asked.

"My good man, we have the perfect plan. Just think, we have the girls to do the job."

"We do?" he asked in a whisper, moving close to me.

"Yes we do, for that kind of a reward I know three young ladies that would trim the toe nails on a mountain lion."

"Are you talking about Mary, Susie, and Ruby?"

"That's right; I'll take care of Jessie, or whatever his real name is."

Chapter Nineteen

I could tell that Arthur was just a little skeptical about the whole ordeal; he had heard what the Pinkerton Agents had said about the outlaws on our wagon train. What I needed to do now was to gather up the three ladies and give them the word and the plan about Mae Bell and her boy friend.

After supper when everything had settled down, I managed to get the ladies all in one wad. "I know you want to know what the two strangers were doing here earlier, talking to me and Arthur. Well listen, before you start asking questions. You ladies were right about Jessie and Julie; they are outlaws and very dangerous... wait, wait, now before you start talking. The two men in suits were Pinkerton Agents, and they tell me the dangerous duo has a sizeable reward on their head. Needless to say, this is where you ladies come in." I took the hand-cuffs out of my pocket and held them up. The three girls began to look at each other, as if I was joking.

"Go on..." Mary said.

"Well, all you three need to do is put the hand-cuffs on Mae Bell; That's right, Mae Bell Davis, the notorious outlaw and murderer from Illinois."

"How much did you say the reward was?" Susie asked, smiling.

"I didn't say, but I imagine it will be ten thousand or more." The girls looked back and forth at one and the other.

"We can do it! I'm sure we can do it, three against one woman; we can do it," stated Ruby, her eyes sparkling.

"Now here's one more thing, the Pinkerton Agents said she has sixty thousand dollars in her possession, so keep this in mind. I doubt she will want to give this up for a hanging or prison sentence. One other thing, she may have a derringer close by her side...probably concealed."

"How do you suppose we go about this venture without getting hurt?" Mary asked. The girls took notice and nodded.

"As I said, Arthur plans on going through Sage, Texas about one or two o'clock tomorrow. I'll call Jessie over to our wagon to help me do something, and you ladies go over to her wagon and call her out to ask her a question. This is where you three surprise her. I suggest y'all get her down and put her hands behind her back, then put the hand-cuffs on her." The girls nodded in agreement, looking at each other.

"Piece of cake," said Susie. I started laughing.

"What seems to be so funny?" Mary asked with a smirk of a smile.

"Oh, I was just wondering if I was going to get a cup of coffee with that piece of cake Susie had."

"I'll tell you what you gonna get Bill Allen, if you get us hurt." Then we all started laughing.

"You're not talking about knots about my head and shoulders, are you?" I asked, as I grabbed Mary and started goosing her.

"We could do it, couldn't we Susie and Ruby?" asserted Mary, looking at the others.

"You know what I think?"

"No, what do you think, my darling Bill Allen?"

"I think you ladies are getting just too big for your britches. But I sure was impressed the way you made sport out of the McCurry brothers. I'll be the first to admit that took lots of faith in your own skill in drawing and fanning a Colt. I really didn't know you ladies were all that fast with a six gun."

"There is a lot you don't know about us, isn't there, ladies?"

"Well there probably is, but, if you will put up the curtain between us and this bunch of sharp-shooters, I'm going to bed." I was sure Mary, Susie and Ruby would sleep on pins and needles tonight just knowing the task before them tomorrow. Then, the other aspect of the whole thing was...they would be responsible for the apprehending of Mae Bell and her going to prison or being hung. I knew personally this would happen, I had killed many a men in my short life and it didn't get any easier.

According to Arthur we were going to go through Sage, Texas about mid day, give or take an hour. The wagon train had gotten off to a good start; we were making good time - the road was smooth and dry for a change. We had decided to apprehend our outlaws when we stopped in Sage. We knew the Pinkerton Agents would be at the saloon. This is where we could turn them over and make the transition. I just figured that Jessie and, Julie, better known as Mae Bell Davis, would keep a low profile while we were in the town of Sage. I presumed the ladies were biding their time and wondering just how they were going to apprehend this fugitive from justice without someone getting shot. I had my own chore to perform with Jessie - as Susie implied 'a piece of cake'. As we passed the city limit sign of Sage, Texas, Arthur started looking for a place to camp for the night. Several folk needed supplies and hoped to stock up before going on.

The girls were watching me like a hawk when I walked over to Jessie and Julie's wagon and called him out to help me. I had already conversed with Larry Morris and told him what was going down, and who Jessie and Julie Parks really were. As far as we knew, they were the ones that had stolen the pictures and plates. But the plan turned around on them, and Mae Bell's picture managed to get in all the newspapers all over the country, and she was recognized by folks in the places she had robbed. What was that phrase someone coined: 'you give a monkey too much grapevine and he will hang himself'?

I slapped on the side of Jessie's wagon. "Hey man, are you awake this morning?" I called out. The three girls were looking on, but laying low, back at our wagon, getting ready to pounce upon Mae Bell.

"Just a minute, Bill, let me get my boots on. I'm just a little under the weather, and Julie, too."

"I noticed you all didn't come over for breakfast this morning." Finally he moved the back covering to his wagon, enough to stick his head out.

"What is it you're wanting this morning, Bill?"

"Well I thought maybe you would ride with me over to the feed store this morning. Since I don't have ol' Ray to help me, you and I could stock upon some grain for the horses, since we are kinda running low. We can take the buckboard and be back in no time."

"Let me talk it over with Julie and see what her plans are for today and see if she needs anything from town."

Personally I thought the man was stalling; there was no way he knew my intentions this morning. I wonder now - did he or Julie, by any chance, happen to see the Pinkerton Agents over here talking to me and Arthur Gates.

"She said she didn't have any plans and it would be okay, anyway I could help, I'll be right there."

"That's fine. meet me down at the buckboard," I answered, as I walked off. I was waiting at the wagon when Jessie walked up. I guess he could see that I didn't even have the horses harnessed up to the wagon. And I could see he wasn't wearing a pistol, but might have a loaded Derringer in his pocket. I flipped the thong off the hammer of my trusty Colt, just in case I had to use it on Jessie.

"I guess you want me to help you harness up the horses?"

"Firs,t we need to talk Jessie, and this could be a very touchy subject." I could tell he was taken by surprise and somewhat caught off guard.

"I have money, if you want me to help out with the feed bill," he said, standing at the back of the wagon looking at the few sacks of grain we still had left.

"No, Jessie, it is a little more complex." I think now he thought I was on to something more than going to get feed for the horses. "I want to talk to you about your wife."

"My wife!" he exclaimed, "what about my wife?"

"Well for starters, Jessie, the girls don't think Julie is your wife, and it appears she is much older than you." I could tell that struck a nerve.

"Now just what business is that to them?" He said, with a growing attitude.

"None I suppose...and one other thing, they don't think she is pregnant." I could tell now Jessie knew I was on to something.

"I say again, that is none of their business what me and Julie do or do not do," by now Jessie was getting a little huffy.

"Well, I think it is some of their business when they are traveling with a lying woman that is a fugitive from the law."

Jessie's face began to turn to red, "You wait one minute, Bill Allen, don't you tie me up with that woman; I only met her in Bessemer, Alabama, and she hired me to drive a wagon. I don't know if she is with child or not; if she is, it damn shore ain't mine."

"I bet you don't know she has killed at least three men, and robbed banks from Illinois to Tennessee." By this time Larry Morris had walked up to where Jessie and I were talking. I handed Larry a pair of hand-cuffs. "Cuff him, Larry. If you are innocent you will walk free; but you are going into town this morning to give an account to the Pinkerton Agents that are waiting on you." I guess he knew his running days were over with Mae Bell Davis. He stuck his arms out for Larry to put the cuffs on his hands, like a sheep being led to slaughter.

"What are you going to do with Julie?" Jessie asked.

"Do you know her real name is Mae Bell Davis, and she's from Iowa?"

"Look, Bill, I'm glad I am caught; I am tired of lying for her."

I took Jessie by the arm and headed up to where the girls and Mae Bell were. As I neared his wagon I couldn't believe my eyes; there stood Mae Bell Davis with both hands cuffed behind her back. Nasty and dirty wouldn't describe her. All the girls were in the same shape - hair hanging down in their face, clothes ripped, and some blood on their noses and lips. Poor ole Mae Bell looked like she had been in a hatchet fight, and everyone had a hatchet but her.

"What happened?" I asked.

"Don't even ask," Mary answered.

"But..."

"But is right. Have you ever tried sticking wet spaghetti up a wildcat's butt?" Ruby asked. It wasn't funny, but I had to laugh.

"Okay, Mae Bell, you and Jessie are going over to see the Pinkerton Agents; they should be over in the saloon, about now, waiting on us. Oh, by the way, they said you might as well bring the money you stole, from all the banks you robbed."

Mae Bell turned and looked at me as if I was out of my mind. "They got me, but they will never get the money."

"Jessie, you might as well go and get the money out of your wagon. It will help matters for you," I recommended.

I could see a smirk on Mae Bell's face. "He doesn't know where the money is; no one knows what I did with the money."

"Did you ever see the money, Jessie?" I asked.

"Oh yes, I have seen it several times; but I haven't seen it lately."

"Now, Mae Bell Davis, you might as well fess up and tell us where you hid the money. The law might take the recovery of the money into consideration at your trial."

"I know my destination. I will never go to prison; I'll be buried with all my money," was her reply.

It was several days later I understood what Mae Bell meant. Oh well, it was sad for some, but a happy day for others. The reward money, and the two hundred I had given Gloria, was burning the girls' pockets. Maggie Lofton left the two boys with their grandpa, and they all went shopping in Sage.

"Now ladies, don't forget to buy plenty of ammunition for the pistols; I want Maggie and Gloria to practice and get as good as you are Ruby."

"What about me, Mr. Bill? I'm as fast as Ruby," Susie said.

"Yes, and what about me?" Mary questioned. I knew I had stuck my foot in my mouth by bragging on one and not the other.

"Okay, okay, you girls keep on practicing. We will have a shooting contest just as soon as y'all teach Maggie and Gloria to draw and shoot. We all replenished our supplies; the ladies bought new clothes, while Jessie and Mae Bell were locked behind bars, in the local jail.

That night, as Mary, Susie, and Ruby sat in the back of the wagon dividing their reward money, by the coal-oil lantern light, I was in bed trying to figure out where Mae Bell could have hidden all that bank robbery money. I remembered what she said just after the girls had managed to get the hand-cuffs on her... 'I know my destination, I will never go to prison, and I'll be buried with all my money.' I'll be buried with all my money; just what did she mean by that? I'll be buried with all my money?"

The next morning, bright and early, Arthur was knocking on the side of my wagon. "Hold on a minute, I'm coming out." The girls were already dressed and gone.

"What are we going to do with the Park's wagon setting up there in front of you?"

I finished tying my holster to my leg. "To tell you the truth, I hadn't thought about it." I said.

"Well, we could take it with us, no telling when one of our wagons may break down," stated Arthur:

"Good point, but ain't we just about got more wagons than we got drivers fer 'em?"

"Remember now, we could use extra water; I hear it gets mighty dry in Texas, and we could get some more water barrels before we leave Sage." While Arthur and I were discussing the extra wagon, we saw Jessie walking our way.

"Don't shoot; I didn't break-out of jail!" he said in a loud tone of voice.

"Me and Arthur were just discussing your wagon. What are you doing here?"

"They turned me loose, when I got through telling my story; the Pinkerton Agents didn't have anything on me. Driving a wagon from Bessemer, Alabama to Sage, Texas isn't against the law. But y'all ain't going to believe what happened somewhere between midnight and daylight this morning!"

I looked at Arthur, and we both shook our heads. "Try us," I said, "I'll believe most anything now days."

"Mae Bell killed herself!"

"You have got to be pulling our leg, man, there ain't any way. How did Mae Bell kill herself?" Arthur asked.

"As you know, we were put in the local jail and questioned for the longest. I was actually turned loose last night, but I had a warm bed – even if it wasn't too comfortable. They fed me supper last night and breakfast this morning and said I could go anytime; the cell door was open."

Chapter Twenty

"Well getting' back to Mae Bell, you said she took her own life?"

"Yes, as I was saying, I was in a different cell than Mae Bell...but I could hear what was going on. It was about midnight when Mae Bell called to the night jailer and asked for a glass of water. It was no trouble hearing him mumble and grumble coming to the cell. But anyhow, he brought her a can of water and told her to be quiet the rest of the night, folks were trying to sleep. And that was the last word I heard until the hoopla this morning. The Pinkerton Agents came to question her about where she hid the bank money. Well lo and behold, she was piled up in her bunk dead as a door nail, and done stiff as a board."

"Surely she wasn't shot; you would have heard the noise," Arthur commented.

"And I gather she didn't hang herself, so what happened?" I asked.

"The first thing the Pinkerton Agents did was come to the next cell and wake me up and begin to question me, as if I knew something. They said it's for sure she didn't have a heart attack or she would have called to the jailer again. The only thing I knew I could tell them that might help was that Mae Bell always wore a gold chain around her neck with a locket in the shape of a heart. She was very particular about the thing; she wore it night and day and took it off only when she took a bath. I just thought for the longest it was a picture of her mother and father, or a child maybe. Well, one day a few months back, she was in the tub taking a bath and asked me to get her some more hot water. And I guess the curiosity that killed the cat got the best of me. Her robe and slippers were lying on a table near by, along with the heart-shaped locket. She wasn't looking so I popped it open, and the only thing in the locket was a capsule. I snapped it back and never questioned her. I knew she had some peculiar ways and I never asked her many questions. The Pinkerton Agents rushed to her cell to find the locket open and the capsule missing. It was a cyanide tablet, I heard the Pinkerton man say. I put on my hat and walked out of the jail and Mae Bell's life."

"Are you going to stick around for the funeral?" I asked.

"No, but I would like to go on with the wagon train, if y'all will have me. I've got money to pay my way. I don't have the sixty thousand dollars or any idea what Mae Bell did with it. As she said, it is buried with her."

I looked at Arthur. He smiled and said, "At least we have a driver for our water wagon."

We explained to Jessie about needing more water for the horses. He was more than glad to let us put extra water barrels on his wagon.

I had plenty of money and was getting the reward for the Benson Gang, but to let sixty thousand dollars rot in the ground was more than I could take.

"A penny for your thoughts," Mary remarked, as she lay there beside me.

"You really want to know?" I asked, rolling over her way on our homemade mattress. "I was thinking about that sixty thousand dollars Mae Bell had, and how she could have gotten rid of it. Haven't you given it any thought?"

"Well, yes, but that's about as far as it got; I found out I don't worry about things I can't do anything about."

"I'm about the same way, but I believe we can do something about finding that money. Do you remember what she said? 'That money will be buried with me'. Oh well, we both know the money wasn't buried with her; she never had the money when we carried her over to the Pinkerton Agents."

"That's right," Mary said, then asked, "So how was the money buried with her?" I put my arms around Mary and pulled her close.

"In her head, only in her head, she knew where she hid the money. Now we both know she couldn't leave it just lying around someplace, so she buried it. And I believe she buried it before she knew she was going to get caught."

"I still think it's a needle in a hay stack," Mary answered, putting her arms around my neck.

"But with a strong magnet one can find a needle in a hay stack, can't they?"

Mary took a long breath and sort of wiggled up to me. "I guess they could, if you say so, what's a dumb magnet?"

"Mary, honey, it's a horse shoe looking thing that is magnetized, and will pick up nails without touching them.

"In other words, you're implying that with a good, strong determination you can find that pile of money?" Mary asked, about to go to sleep.

"Think back with me before you go to sleep; you remember the evening you girls shot the Benson Gang, and later on they were buried, down the road from where we were camped?"

"Yes, I remember that," Mary yawned, "and Larry Morris made pictures of us standing behind the Benson Gang, what about it?"

"Now the way I got it figured, it was so much going on no one was watching what the other were doing. Don't you think it would have been mighty easy for Mae Bell to drop the sixty thousand dollars in one of the graves?" I questioned, giving Mary a kiss.

"You know, it was dark by the time the bodies were covered up," Mary replied, "And she was afraid the local law would be sneaking around asking questions."

"I believe you are right, Mary, she could have eased over to their wagon without anyone noticing. It would have been mighty easy for to bring the bag of money back to the grave...without Jessie even noticing her."

"That's right, I'm sure the money was in a canvas bag. I also believe she would have come back for the money, after everything settled down." I could tell I had talked my true love to sleep. I thought - its worth a look see, sixty thousand dollars is lots of money to rot in the cold, cold ground.

I managed to get a few winks, but eased up before daylight and woke Mary up. "Just listen," I whispered, "I'm gonna saddle my horse and take a pack horse and a spare, and ride back to where we buried the Benson Gang."

"That will take several days of hard riding, won't it?" she asked.

"Yes, but if I find the money it will be worth it all, don't you think?" Mary started getting up.

"What'cha getting up for?" I asked.

"I am going to pack you some victuals for you to carry with you. Might as well let me help you pack the horses; it won't take that much time and you will need some grub."

I suppose you're right, but don't you tell anybody on the wagon train what my intentions are."

"I'm sure they will ask. Don't forget to pack some extra cover and a shovel to dig with...I wish you were taking me along with you."

"I would, Baby, but you need to be moving along with the wagon train. And whatever you do, you take good care of our wagon while I'm gone."

I was leaving a small fortune in that double bottomed box we were using for a bed. It was just getting daylight when I pulled Mary close and kissed her goodbye.

"I still wish you were carrying me with you, this is the first time you and I have been separated since we met."

I mounted up and was gone before anyone in camp noticed me riding off. I kicked my horse in the ribs and achieved a comfortable gallop, and watched the sun come up in the east as I rode along. I was leading a pack horse, and an extra horse to ride when my horse seemed a wee-bit tired. Going back the way I came was a like reading a book the second time. The only time I stopped the first day was to water the horses, get me a bite of grub, and bed down for the night. I was in the saddle the next morning bright and early, hoping to cover much territory. I know one thing; I wasn't comfortable sleeping on the ground anymore. And I missed the hot meals I had grown accustomed to.

I met many folks going west, even a small wagon train or two. I waved and kept right on riding. It was the third day. I was galloping along dozing in and out, not far from my destination - where we buried the Benson Gang. Right in the middle of the road was a covered wagon with the two lead horses down. The second look I took, I would say they were all but dying.

"Howdy do, mister," I called, bringing my horses to a halt. The middle-aged man was squatting down, looking at his two downed horses He quickly looked around at me.

"Morning to you, young man, sad to say, but I have gotten myself in a fine mess."

I needed a rest and it was about time for a snack, so I eased out of the saddle for a spell to stretch my legs, and hoping to fill the hollow in my gut.

The man had a four horse team; the two horses in the back next to the wagon, were all but falling down.

"It looks like you have been pushing your horses too hard."

"Yes Sir, you could say that, me not knowing much about horses have done just that, don't you think?" It wasn't hard for me to agree with the man, seeing the four starved and dying horses.

"Do you have any plans what you are going to do now? This is a lonely road and people coming by don't render much help."

"Well, the wife and I were just talking, and we really don't know what we will do now since the horses are dying."

"How many are with you?" I asked, looking all around."

"Just my wife and daughter, they are over there in the woods looking for water and something to eat."

I could see right now this bunch of city folks were going to mess up my plans for today. 'For crying out loud', as Mary would say, I couldn't just leave them here stranded with dead horses, and starving to death themselves. . .could I?

"Were you with that wagon train I passed yesterday?" I asked, hearing women's voices coming out of the thicket on the right side of the road."

"No sir, but we were in hot pursuit to catch up to them. You see, we have been robbed of all our food and supplies." I wondered about his intentions as I watched a beautiful young girl and her mother walk toward the wagon, carrying an empty bucket and straw basket.

"Did you all find any water?" the man asked. The two ladies hung their heads. "I guess that means no," the man said ,taking the empty bucket and basket. "You two go get in the wagon, maybe this young man can help me think of something."

"Just a minute, before you ladies go, I was just fixing to stop and eat me a bite before I ran into you. Y'all are welcome to eat what I got. I've got extra water on my pack horse also."

The young girl who was in her late teens, I would say, smiled and took a step my way. "Hold it, now!" the man scolded, "the young man will need his provisions for his journey."

I thought to myself...pride and a fool go hand in hand.

"No, I have an ample supply, for all of us, really I do. But first let us get the wagon over there in the shade, next to those trees. The man quickly unhitched the horses and we pushed the wagon back away from them. Then he and I managed to get it off the road, by using the help of my horses.

"By the way, my name is Bill Allen, and I am leading a wagon train into Fort Worth Texas. I had to come back on business. I was nearing my destination when I run up on you folks."

"Well, I'm Josh Dillon and my wife is Sarah, and my daughter is Katie. We are much obliged for your kind generosity and will always be indebted to you."

Mary had packed enough food for me to feed a small army; one thing for sure, she didn't intend on me going hungry. While the woman was searching through my food supply I walked toward the woods to gather up some firewood. When I turned around there stood the young girl.

"Can I help you, Mr. Bill?" she asked in the softest voice I have ever heard, and she began to pick up small, broken branches.

"Oh yes, thank you very much I plan to make us some coffee to drink with our lunch." Strange to say, but the young lady never took her eyes off of me. Her mother and father seemed to not notice, but it was somewhat embarrassing for me, to say the least.

"Do you remember crossing a river, about ten miles back east?"

"Yes, I do. That is where we were robbed - at the river," answered Josh Dillon.

"I'm going to leave my pack horse here with you. I should be back before dark. I will bring back some team horses, that is if I can find any. I eased on over to my horse and started to mount up to go. Just as I put my foot in the stirrup to mount I felt a hand take hold of my arm, I quickly looked around.

"Can I go with you, Mr. Bill?" The young lady asked. Her eyes were just sparkling. I took my foot out of the stirrup and turned around to face her. Her body was practically up against mine. "Do you mind if I ride with you on your extra horse?"

I thought - this is complicating things a bit. "I don't mind if your folks don't, can you ride?"

"No, but you can teach me, can't you, Mr. Bill?"

I could tell now this beautiful, blond headed girl had taken an overly passionate interest in me, and that wasn't the best path of wisdom.

"Look Katie, let me go by myself. I will be back before dark; I can make better time by myself."

She hung her head and backed up for me to mount up and leave.

Katie waved at me as I rode off holding the reins of the spare horse. I rode pretty hard until I reached the river; the horses were ready for a drink, and I was ready for a break. The river was overflowing out of its banks, but I had no trouble crossing. I knew the graves were just ahead ,but didn't know what to expect or where to start.

I dismounted and tied the horses to a low hanging branch. I untied the shovel I had brought and walked over to the graves. I thought to myself, I'll do my eeny-meeny-miney-mo and start digging. But as I stood there surveying the graves, I noticed one was somewhat different...different, as to say, it had rocks piled at the head and foot of the grave. I was somewhat like the fly that fell in the churn full of cream; I didn't quite know where to start. I was hoping this wouldn't be a needle in a hay stack thing. I moved the rocks from the foot of the grave and started digging. I knew I was down deep enough to come in contact with the body. I thought I had hit it, but as I started moving the dirt around in the foot of the grave, I found a canvas bag. And the bag was full of money.

Chapter Twenty-one

I carefully packed my two large saddle bags full of money. I threw the canvas bag back in the grave and covered it with dirt. I tied my shovel and bed roll behind the saddle, good and tight, and started for the river. One mission accomplished - I just might be pressing my luck to find Josh Dillon some horses - were the thoughts running through my head. as I crossed the river and started back to his wagon.

I reckoned I had ridden four or five miles when I saw a sign pointing down a three track road; I hadn't noticed this sign when I came this way a week ago. J & J RANCH the sign read. I might be in luck after all. I definitely had the money, if they had some horses. With nothing to lose I ventured down the road and soon spied a house and a windmill. As I rode up several barking dogs ran out from under the house. I pulled the horses up to a dilapidated picket fence with the gate torn mostly off its hinges.

"Hello!" I called out, as loud as I could. As I waited I saw two men coming from a barn a ways down behind the farmhouse. Just before they reached me. I dismounted.

"Good day, young fellow, how can I help you?" asked the older man. Standing in the background was a young boy.

"I'm in dire need of some horses to pull a covered wagon."

The man took off his hat and wiped his forehead on his sleeve. "I got some, but I doubt you want to pay the price fer 'em."

"Don't judge a book by its cover, Mister, I don't look like much, but I got a smidgen of money."

"It's gonna take more than a little money to get them horses down there," he said as he pointed. "I been asking seventy five dollars a head fer 'em, 'course ain't nobody got money since the war."

"You drive a hard bargain, Mister, but I'll pay it if they will pull a wagon."

"That's what they're trained for, is to pull a wagon. Say...you wouldn't need this boy would you? He's looking for a job."

"Now that you mention it, I do need some help. What can you do? My name is Bill Allen, what's yours?"

"My name is James...James Sawyer, I'm just passing through and stopped to see if this man needed some help, I'm heading west."

"Can you shoot a pistol and handle a Henry?"

"I guess I could, if I had one."

"Well you're hired, twenty five dollars a month, a place to sleep and all you can eat. Now go get me those four horses while I pay the man." It wasn't long before James and I were leading four team horses en route to the wagon where I had left my pack horse. "Where do you hail from, James? You said you were just passing through."

"I'm an Alabama boy, from Selma. Just down on my luck; don't have no where to go but up and west."

"I don't believe I have ever heard it put that way, but you are in luck, I'm heading west, as far as Fort Worth, Texas."

"Well now, Mr. Bill, I'm already glad I ran up with you."

"One other thing James, don't ever call me mister again, do you hear what I'm saying?"

"Oh, I hear, okay, I was just doing it out of respect; you do have a few years on me, I'm just going on seventeen."

"Well, I'll be twenty next week, and I feel like I'm forty." I reckoned we were about five miles from our destination, hoping to get Josh Dillon back rolling again.

"You see what I see up there in the road?" James asked, sitting up in the saddle stretching his neck.

"Yeah, I do, and it could be the oldest trick in the book, just watch yourself."

There stood two horses and a man sprawled out in the middle of the dirt road. The second man was bent over him as if he were trying to administer help, or help him get up.

James and I pulled up and got all the horses stopped and calmed down. "What seems to be the trouble here, mister?" I asked the man, who seemed to be trying to help his companion.

"Don't really know as of yet, I just have rode up and found this man lying in the middle of the road. You might give me a hand. I don't know if he is dead or alive."

When I dismounted I was on the blind side of the man, and my horse was between him and me.

"Watch him, Bill he's pulled a gun on you!" James shouted still sitting on his horse. Well, instead of me walking around in front of my horse and getting shot, I drew my pistol, dropped to my knees, and shot from under my horse. By the time I filled him full of lead, the man laying on the ground had rolled over and pulled his gun on me. I quickly fanned three shots in his direction; well, I'm sad to say, there lay two men lying in the middle of the road shot full of holes. Their only intentions were to rob and probably kill us, and leave us lying in the middle of the road.

As James dismounted and walked to where the men were lying, he noticed one of the men wasn't dead but was moving his mouth, trying to talk. We both rushed to his side. and James lifted him up so he could breathe much easier.

"I wasn't gonna kill y'all," said the man, as he lay on the ground with blood running from his mouth. "Me and Curtis was just gonna take the horses back up the road, and sell them to the man with the dead horses.

"You and Curtis wasn't going to sell the man up the road anything, he has no money," I declared to the dying man..

"Curtis said he would trade the four horses for that pretty little blonde filly that was smiling at us when we stopped." He coughed several times. "The man said he had help coming. So me and Curtis decided to wait on you." And with those words the man's head dropped, and he died. James laid him down on the road and looked at me.

"I thought we were goners there for a minute, didn't you, Bill?"

"No! It never crossed my mind. Those two rednecks probably couldn't hit the side of the barn if they were inside of the barn, anyway."

"He said he wasn't planning on killing us, didn't he?" James queried, as he stood up.

"Well now, James, how was I supposed to know that, and what was he gonna do with the pistol pointed at me...scratch my back?" I walked back over to my horse and untied the shovel from my bed roll. James was watching me like a hawk. "Give me a hand with this man." I picked up one arm and James caught hold of the other. "Let's drag him out here in the woods and plant him, so the buzzards don't pick his bones." I started digging a hole in the ground. It seemed soft enough that this venture would not take all evening. James walked back over and caught the other man by a hand full of collar and dragged him over where I was still digging. "Did you say you didn't have a gun rigging?" I asked James.

"No sir, but it looks like this character is wearing a brand new Colt and holster. It seems a shame to roll him over in that hole and cover it up, wouldn't you say?" I propped up on the shovel.

"I would definitely say that, if I didn't have a pistol and holster."

"It sounds as if you would be in complete agreement if I relieve this scum bag of his hardware."

"You are plowing pretty close to my corn, James, and I would relieve the other man of his rigging and use it for a spare…and while we're on the subject, I noticed a good looking Henry rifle in his scabbard on his horse over there."

"You don't reckon, they'll mind do you?"

"Well you can ask them before you make a rash move. If I was you I would check their pockets; if they have any money on them you can have it." That idea, seemed to impress James as he began scavenging through the men's pockets.

"Well, this'un had forty dollars on him."

"Well, roll 'em in the hole, and check the other man."

"This'un has got nearly sixty dollars on him."

"Well, roll him in the hole."

"You want both of them in the same hole?" James questioned, a bit hesitantly.

"I don't hear them complaining, do you?"

"You want me to cover them up? You dug the hole."

"Believe it or not, James, you took the words right out of my mouth." I threw the shovel to James and sat down to rest and watch.

By the time James and I made it back to the wagon where the Dillon family was waiting, it was late in the evening, and really too late to hitch up the team. Josh Dillon had taken it on himself to tie the two living horses in some good grass - probably saving their lives. There was no hope for the ones that had fallen.

"James, take the team horses and drag the two dead horses down the road from where we are camping, and shoot 'em in the head to make sure they are dead. I'm going to scout us up some supper: The girl will help you scare up some wood for a fire tonight, if you ask her." I turned around and started through the woods just west of the camp, hoping to find a deer. I thought, beggars can't be choosy - a wild hog would do, Lord. I took out my Henry, loaded a cartridge in the chamber, and got ready.

What I saw wasn't a deer or wild hog, but better. I actually had to do a double take to believe what I was looking at - a half grown calf, as healthy as the day is long. I did my hoot owl thing, and the calf looked right at me. I touched the trigger, and the rest is history. There were some surprised folks at the camp when I came dragging a calf to be butchered.

James and Katie had a rip-roaring fire going and Sarah was getting out a skillet. All I can say is, if everyone didn't get a bite of tender steak, it was their own fault.

The next morning, with the coals still hot as blue blazes, Sarah fried up some more tender steaks and a couple of hoecakes. With a pot of fresh coffee, it couldn't get any better. With the fresh horses we were on our way, and hoped to pull into Platt, Louisiana before dark. We forded several small creeks and stopped to fill the barrel on the wagon with water, and to let the horses drink, without losing much time. After the horses drank their fill we were on our way. Katie thought she was something, riding along with James on her own horse. Thank God, he got her out of my hair; if Mary even thought I looked at that little blonde she would scratch my eyes out, or do worse. I rode over to Josh and Sarah's wagon .

"When we get to Platt, pull right up in front of the general store and we'll load up."

Sarah took her husband by the arm, "Josh, did you tell Bill we don't have any money we were robbed?" He looked at me.

"Bill, you did enough for us, the horses must have cost you a fortune. The wife has some jewelry her mother gave her; we can sell it and get a few dollars for groceries."

Nothing I had ever heard touched me as this did. Here I sat in front of two saddlebags with sixty thousand dollars in them, and this woman was going to part with the only thing her mother had given her, for a few supplies.

"Do you folks believe in miracles?" I asked. They both looked at each other.

"We sure do!" Sarah exclaimed.

"Well, when we pass the Platt city limit sign, Mrs. Sarah, if you will look in the back of your wagon, you will find a blessing. Now don't look back until we pass the sign. I'm gonna check on the horses back there and see if they are doing okay."

Before I rode back behind the wagon I rode up to where James and Katie were having themselves a ball. "Are you two doing alright?" I asked, just making conservation, as I unbuckled the straps on one of my saddle bags and took out a bundle of bills, unbeknown to anyone. I stuck it under my leg and buckled the straps back, I nonchalantly made my way back to where the horses were tied to the back of the wagon.. I tossed the bundle of bills in the back of the wagon and rode back up to where Josh was holding the reins of his team, and remarked, "I believe the horses are going to be alright when we get them some grain to supplement their grass."

I rode past the Platt city limit sign and watched to see if Sarah would get up and go to the back of their wagon; as soon as they passed the sign she didn't lose any time heading that way. I waited, but she didn't come back to the seat; instead, Josh halted the horses, set the brake on the wagon, and disappeared into the back of the wagon. I waited and waited. I thought, this is ridiculous, and decided I would ride back to the wagon. As I neared the wagon I could tell there was a prayer meeting going on. A warm feeling came up in the pit of my stomach.

I don't believe they even noticed me coming and going. I was sitting in front of the general store when Josh and Sarah pulled up. Josh slowly stepped down and helped Sarah to the ground. I guess James and Katie was already in the store; I knew that money was burning a hole in his pocket. Sure enough, there they stood over in one corner, eating candy. I stood at the door and waited on Sarah and Josh to come in, to see what they were going to say about the bundle of bills. Well, instead of saying anything about the money she turned quickly and went back out on the board walk…I thought, this is mighty strange, and stepped back outside to see what was the matter with Mrs. Sarah.

"What is it, Mrs. Sarah?"

She caught me by the shoulder and began to point with her finger in a pecking motion. "The man at the counter with the two Indians is the bunch that robbed us yesterday at the river."

"Are you sure?" I asked.

147

"She is right, Bill. I would know that bunch in the dark."

I flipped the thong off my Colt and jobbed it up and down in my holster several times to make sure it wasn't stuck.

"Come on back in the store, but don't get between me and the man you said robbed y'all."

Evidently the man and the two half breeds hadn't noticed Sarah and Josh in the store, standing to one side.

"Pardon me one minute, sir, this lady and gentlemen tells me that you stopped by their covered wagon yesterday and took most of their provisions, and four hundred dollars they had saved to go west. In other words, you son-of-a bitch, you and these two lazy, dead-beat half breeds left this family to die."

"Now you wait just one minute, boy," said the man at the counter. I saw him fixing to go for his pistol. I drew mine at lightning speed and put the barrel up against his temple.

"No, you wait just one minute before I let in some daylight to your brain." I cut my eye over to one side, "Come over here, Mrs. Sarah." She quickly looked at her husband standing close by her side, he nodded. And she eased over to where I was standing. "Mrs. Sarah, you take a good look... What was these buzzards driving or riding when they robbed you and your husband?"

She backed up a step, adjusted her specs, and cocked her head.

"Those two Indians were driving the buckboard, the one sitting outside. And this man was riding a horse - the same one that is tied up to the rail behind the buckboard; I would know that horse and fancy saddle anywhere," she answered and moved back.

"I tell you what...you go outside and look in the buckboard and see if any of your stuff is still in the wagon." I could tell the man was a bit uncomfortable. "You hold still now," I commanded. I pushed the barrel of my pistol up and down the side of his ugly face. "If you even smile, mister, I'll shoot you dead." It became as quiet as a prayer meeting. Mrs. Sarah returned, white as a sheet, wringing her hands.

"It is all my stuff, even to my pots and pans they took."

"Now, what have you got to say for yourself, you maggot, take everything out of your pocket and lay it on the counter." He hesitated for a thought..."Now!!!!" I cocked my Colt, "Mister, I'm just before blowing your head off even with your shoulders." He began to clean his pockets; the last thing he laid on the counter was a roll of hard earned cash. I picked the roll of money up and handed to Sarah to inspect. "Count it," I said.

She reached for the roll of money and began to thumb through the bills, counting. She looked up at me and made eye contact. "It's all here, four hundred dollars, and it still has the scent of cedar, where I have kept it in my cedar chest all these years."

"From now on, you and your half-breeds need to be more particular who you rob." I holstered my pistol and turned to walk out of the store, taking a chance, I know, but my blood was boiling, and this man needed killing.

I was nearly at the door when Mrs. Sarah shouted, "He's going for his gun, Bill!" I dropped to the floor, rolled over, got my finger on the trigger, and sat up fanning my Colt. My first shot was right between his eyes. He staggered back, knocking over a cracker barrel, and wilted to the floor.

"James, get over here! Get these two wooden Indians to help you drag this slime out in the street; he is bleeding all over the floor," I announced in a bitter tone of voice, getting to my feet. By this time the shot had attracted some onlookers, because as usual, everybody loves a circus. But I was growing just a little tired of being judge, jury and executioner.

Two days had passed, and I had killed three men. I fought in the Civil War for two years. That war was over, but was the war in me over? Some man touched my arm and I turned around to see who it was.

"Sir, I am the store owner. You have done the town of Platt a great service today by killing Phil Done; he was a menace to society; a trouble maker from the word go."

As I thanked the man, I thought, it does make me feel somewhat better to have shot someone that needed killing. But since he was a trouble maker and a menace to society 'why ain't somebody done killed him'?

Chapter Twenty-two

I walked over to where Mr. and Mrs. Dillon, still astonished by what went on, were standing.

"Bill, I want to thank you for getting our money back." Mrs. Sarah opened up her pocket book and took out the stack of bills I had thrown in the back of their wagon earlier. She continued speaking, "Josh and I have talked it over and we must give you this money back, we know you must have put it in the back of our wagon."

"No! Never! I will not hear of it. If you want to do something for me, just never tell anybody you have that much money, or where it came from."

Sarah stood there looking at her husband and said, "God does answer prayer." Then she turned her head and broke down into sobs.

I guess being an answer to someone's prayer smooths the playing field, and makes life worth living for me. I knew one thing, I wanted to get the show on the road and get back to Mary and my own wagon train.

James and Katie were carrying supplies out to the wagon and buckboard as fast as Sarah and Josh were buying it. There is one thing for sure, they would not be lacking between Platt and Fort Worth Texas. I had already talked to them about homesteading somewhere close to our spread so he could farm. I figured the thousand dollars I gave them was a good grubstake to buy seed, and farm supplies, such as plows and harrows.

I was hoping I could trust James to help the Dillons find their way to Fort Worth. And I was sure that he and Katie would get along together...well, not too together.

As we finished loading and were ready to leave the general store, two covered wagons pulled up behind Mr. and Mrs. Dillon. A man, of forty years or so, sailed off the wagon and hailed Mr. Dillon.

"Could I have a word with you, sir?" the man asked.

Mr. Dillon halted his team to see what the man wanted.

"My name is Marvin Travis, and I wonder if you folks are going west?" While the man was waiting on an answer, a young boy, about twelve, walked up beside the man; I supposed it to be his dad. I had already mounted up and was sitting off to one side, but could hear the conservation.

"Well yes, sir, we are. My name is Josh Dillon, and we're hoping to get to Fort Worth and build a cabin before winter."

"We were hoping to run up with a wagon or more going west; I hear tell this is no trail for loners."

"Well, Marvin, you can take it from a believer...we were robbed yesterday; and that dead man, lying over by that cottonwood, is the one that did it."

"I'm not by myself Mr. Dillon, my brother-in-law is in the wagon behind me; his name is Doug Browder."

Mr. Dillon looked over my way, "What do you think, Bill?"

"I say the more the merrier, and he is right, you probably wouldn't have been robbed yesterday if there had been three wagons."

"This is my boy, he is twelve years old and can handle this team as well as me; his name is Jude," said Marvin.

"Well, Jude, it is good to have you going west with us. Why don't you hop on that buckboard and follow Mr. Dillon... we plan to camp not far from here. And you folks are in for a treat tonight; we are having young, tender steak for supper.

After we pulled up the wagons and strung the horses to graze, James and Katie got a rip-snorting fire started and the ladies brought out the Dutch ovens and cast iron skillets. Somebody in the crowd had an ole blue, granite coffee pot that would make enough coffee for a regiment of rebels.

At supper Marvin and his brother-in-law admitted they had never enjoyed steak as much as they had tonight. I told them they were just hungry from the long drive, and even possum would have won them over. We all had a good laugh. Marvin told us that he and his brother-in-law, Doug, had been in the meat processing and packing business

151

in Montgomery, Alabama. During and after the war it was impossible to make a living, since all the beef cattle had been depleted by the long drawn out war between the North and South."

"How are you men at handling a firearm?" I asked.

"Well, Doug is better than I am, but we both can handle ourselves when it comes to trouble. I guess you could say we are good as the next man with a pistol," Marvin said.

"Good as the next man, you say? That type of mentality will only get you in boot hill quicker." The two men looked at each other with a puzzled expression, as I went on, "You have got to be better than the next man, shooting at a person holding a gun is not a game of chance; never gamble, make certain you are holding a sure thing. You must know that you know you can outdraw and out shoot your opponent." I could tell the men understood my point.

"I don't want to scare anyone this evening, but I will be gone in the morning. As you all know now, I have a wagon train about a week's traveling from here, and I need to get back. Like I said before, I don't want to scare anyone, but trouble seems to follow wagon trains, for some reason. Now after I added two and two, this is the reason...all the hungry, lazy, trifling, low life scum-bums thrive on wagon trains heading west. This is easy pickings for them. Most wagon trains have no idea how vulnerable they are; and most have no protection with them. Some have a gun but don't know how to use it." I could see I was making some of the women uncomfortable.

Some of the new people that had just joined the wagon train walked over closer to where I was standing.

"Bill, is it really as bad as you make it to be?" Doug Browder asked. His family was one of the new ones that had joined up.

"Let Josh Dillon answer that, go ahead Josh, you tell 'em."

"All I got to say, you better listen to Bill, I'm lucky to be alive. The wife and daughter had just crossed the river, the big one you all forded a ways back. Lo and behold, we met this bunch of robbers, I didn't know their intentions when I pulled up the horses to a stop. 'Good day, gentleman,' I said, to the big man sitting in a fancy saddle on a solid black horse. There were two Indians sitting on the seat of a buckboard behind him. They were very dark and high-cheeked, and never said a word.

'I'm afraid this will not be a good day for you, Sir' he said, and pulled his rifle out of a scabbard, and breached a cartridge in the chamber. I couldn't believe my eyes, and then he trained it right at my wife Sarah, who was sitting on the wagon seat right beside me. My daughter, Katie, was in the back of the wagon reading. The man said something in Indian language, which I didn't understand. They immediately pulled their buckboard right behind our wagon. All we could do was watch as they began to take our supplies. It scared Katie almost into hysterics; she jumped up in the front of the wagon and sat with us until the Indians got what they wanted out of our wagon. I thought it was all over as the two Indians loaded themselves back on the wagon and started off. The man rode up within touching distance of us.

'I'll take your money now,' he growled, as he waved the rifle barrel at us. The wife quickly reached behind our wagon seat and took out our life savings and handed it to the man. I guess you might say the rest is history, until today when the wife and I patronized the general store in Platt, where we met you all."

"What do you recommend we do to protect ourselves, Bill?" Marvin asked.

"I'm glad you asked that question," I said, and eased over to where the coffee pot was sitting in the hot coals. "First of all, this is not an order or commandment for none of y'all; but the ones that want to get out west better heed my warning, and arm themselves."

"Surely you are not talking about our men wearing a side arm?" one of the ladies sitting over by Marvin asked.

"Are you Marvin's wife?" I asked, as I poured up a cup of coffee and started back to a fold-up chair.

"Yes, I am, my name is Rose."

I stopped dead in my tracks, and turned toward her.

"Yes, that is exactly what I meant: strap on a pistol; and you need to strap on a pistol, too...and learn how to use it. You may save your husband's life, if push comes to shove."

"Well!" she said, "I've heard it all!."

"No Ma'am! You haven't heard it all; let me broaden your intellect. On my wagon train there were five young ladies: Mary, Susie, Ruby, Gloria, and Julie. I told them the same thing I'm telling you. Well, to make a long story short, they strapped on a Colt Pistol and began to practice every time they had a chance. One day, the next week, a mob of men known as the Benson Gang, rode into our camp just before supper, with the intentions to rob and kill all the men, and rape the women. You ladies hear me now...my five ladies were up against twelve outlaws as bad as the James or Dalton Gang. I will never forget this as long as I live...my ladies stepped between the wagons and began shooting their Henry rifles. It sounded like a war, but when the noise died and the smoke cleared, there were a dozen sin-sick misfits sprawled out on the ground dead, and not a one of my girls received a scratch."

"Well Sir," she addressed me "You have very well stated your point, and we do want to start a new life and be free."

"Those who wish to transform the world must be able to transform themselves. The rules and regulations we were accustomed to back east do not apply out west; there is no law and order. Most towns don't even have a sheriff. The Bible says: 'a live dog is worth more than a dead lion' and although the lion is the king of the beasts, he is not very vicious laying dead. So if you want to live free, you must stay alive and prosper." I thought - they can take my advice or leave it; when this bunch shows up in Fort Worth, I'll know they made it.

It was a beautiful day to get started on the long ride back to my wagon train. I had an obligation to the girls and Mary, especially Mary. I know that girl, if I wasn't back when I said I'd be back, she would straddle a horse and come looking for me. I had plenty of everything I needed and more, on my pack horse... including two saddle bags with fifty nine thousand dollars. The question was: Could I make it back with out being robbed, maimed, or killed by some outlaw?

I ate a healthy breakfast before starting on my way back west. I needed something to help pass the time and began to daydream thinking about how I met Mary. I even got tickled remembering myself trimming her finger and toe nails. It seemed just like yesterday I had combed the kinks and knots out of her long hair and let her tell how she got me out of that jail someplace in Alabama. I guess the horses thought I had lost my mind, laughing out loud on this lonesome road, with no one to hear it. She had snatched the whole, dumb wall down; I'd bet that sheriff is still looking for me. It even crossed my mind what I'd do if he found me. It was too fine of a day to dwell on matters like that; I chalked it up as one of those spur of the moment happenings.

Chapter Twenty-three

I know one thing, the nights were getting bitter cold; and sometimes the wind would nearly blow me off my horse. I was sure glad I had brought extra clothes and cover. The wagon train was just a few miles from Fort Worth when I caught up to them. It was dark and most folks were already in bed after a long day's travel. It was a while before Mary sprang the bad news on me. We were lying on our homemade straw mattress. We were about through with our loving, and were getting caught up on how everything went while I was gone.

"I have bad news, my dear!" And I could tell it must be abhorrent, by the way Mary's voice broke.

"What is it, darling?" I asked, pulling her close.

"It's Ruby!"

"Ruby? What's wrong with Ruby?" I asked.

I knew it was bad now.

"Ruby is dead."

"No way!"

"Yes darling, our Ruby is dead." Then Mary really broke.

"Can you tell me how it happened?"

Mary began to regain her composure where she could talk.

"It's not real clear what happened. Let me get a handkerchief to wipe my face."

Mary rolled over and reached for the handkerchief. I gathered her back up in my arms and she went on with what she knew about

Ruby.

"We had camped just west of the town of Keller Point, Texas. As we were looking when we rode through, we noticed the town had a general store and most everything any other small western town would have. Susie said she saw a shoe repair shop on Front Street, and wanted to get her boot fixed. Arthur found a perfect grassy spot for camping, with water nearby. I saw Ruby and Susie head off toward town and never thought anything about it, until an hour later when Susie came tearing into camp and told us that Ruby had been shot to death."

"Did Susie have any idea what might have happened?"

"She said the both of them dismounted and were about to enter the shoe repair shop, but Ruby stopped and was looking at something in the display winders. Anyway, she said she went on in the repair shop and was showing the clerk the broken heel on her boot. A few minutes had passed when she heard a shot fired from outside, never thinking at anytime that Ruby was involved.

She said it was then she noticed a commotion going on outside the shoe repair shop. When she went out to see what all the hoopla was about, she nearly fainted; there was Ruby lying dead in a puddle of her own blood. Someone had already called the sheriff; his office was no more than a rock's throw from where Ruby lay."

"Was there other witnesses present at the time, and did they see what went on?" I asked, getting a bit upset.

"First of all, Bill honey, I wasn't there; and all I know is what the sheriff said, and what Susie was told when she came outside of the shoe shop. There were three Plains Women present who said they seen it all, but right off I knew they were prejudiced and had their own religious agenda; as you know they are 'holier than thou'. They had the gall to say that Ruby brought the whole thing on her self, wearing them tight britches and sporting a gun like a man. As you know, they don't believe in guns, or women in public without their head covered. And they said it was a sin for a woman to wear 'anything that pertaineth to a man', especially women wearing britches."

I lay there listening... getting madder by the minute.

"Arthur and I did get something out of the sheriff...He swore that Ruby pulled a pistol on Ben Turner first, and in self defense he supposedly pulled his pistol on Ruby, and she shot the pistol out of his hand. And according to what the sheriff could get out of the three self righteous Plains Women…they said that Ben Turner's brother, Gladden Turner, was standing near and thought Ruby was going to kill his brother. He, in turn, drew his gun and shot Ruby full of holes."

I just lay listening to Mary, wishing I had been there.

"Well, after we found out that Ben Turner was the sheriff's brother-in-law, we knew that Ruby died in vain. But get this now, after close examination, and what the mortician said at the funeral home, Ruby's blouse was ripped and two buttons were missing. And according to him, Ben Turner had a record of molesting and raping women."

Just hearing that made my blood boil. I thought I might need to do a little investigation work back at Keller Point, Texas and see a sheriff.

"Susie said when she ran out of the shoe repair shop; this Ben Turner was taking on over his hand as if Ruby had shot it off. Well, I'm not going to say what she said, but you can read between the lines. And you really don't want to here what Susie told me."

"I can just imagine."

"She said she started to draw her Colt and shoot all three of 'em, like rabid dogs."

"Well I'm glad she didn't, but I don't feel like justice has been done. I'm going to ride back to the town of Keller Point and look for the two buttons that was torn off of Ruby's blouse."

"Then you feel that Ruby drew her pistol because Ben Turner was molesting her?" Mary questioned.

"Yes, I do, that is why I am going to do a little snooping around when I get to the shoe repair shop. Do you still have the torn blouse that Ruby was wearing the day she got shot?"

"Yes, it is in a bag with her personal stuff, clothes, and gun rigging."

"Good, I need to carry that with me. I'm going to get in touch with the Texas Rangers and let them look into this case also."

The next morning at breakfast I told Arthur I thought I had some unfinished business in Keller Point, Texas. He knew exactly what I was referring too, and nodded in agreement. I decided to carry an extra horse so I could swap up now and then, to keep from running them in the ground.

A little before dinner time the next day I rode into the small town of Keller Point, Texas. It was one of those towns where everybody knew everybody, and strangers weren't welcome. After a few hours I found out they were gonna keep it that way. But money talks and I had brought plenty with me. I first got me a room at the hotel; this sleeping on the hard ground was not my cup of coffee anymore...or was it tea?

My first stop was the shoe repair shop. I crawled around, looking under the boardwalk, in front of the shoe shop. Now I don't mind telling you, I soon drew a crowd, yet no one said anything or asked my name. For a minute I felt like a fool, with only my butt and boots sticking out from under the porch. I guess someone took it upon themselves to go over and make it known to the sheriff that somebody had escaped from the crazy house; and he was right in downtown Keller Point, Texas, crawling around on his hands and knees, sifting sand through his fingers.

"Can I help you there, sonny?" I looked up and there stood a bloated bellied excuse for a man, wearing a badge.

"I guess not, I done found one, and I just reckon the other one should be here close by." The buttons from Ruby's torn blouse had popped off and fallen through the cracks of the boards of the porch. As I suspected, there was the other button.

"What are you doing under the boardwalk, young fellow?"

"I'm looking for buttons, is there a law or town ordinance against it?" I asked, backing out from under the board-walk.

"No! But there is a law against disturbing the peace."

"Well, how could that be? I ain't said nary a word," I replied.

Everyone standing around started laughing, it seemed to irritate the sheriff.

"You don't have to say anything to disturb the peace, boy," the sheriff blurted out, giving the onlookers more to snigger about.

I had already found the two buttons and put them in my shirt pocket. I stood up and announced, "Well, I'm gonna just quit doing whatever I was doing that was disturbing the peace...Sheriff, can you tell me what I was doing that was disturbing the peace, so I wont do it anymore?"

Everybody really busted out and started laughing.

"I tell you what I'm gonna do, boy, if you say one more word I'm gonna lock your smart ass up in the hoosegow. By the way, who are you anyway?" the Sheriff spluttered in rage.

I just stood, tight-lipped and smiling, gazing at the crowd. Everyone was laughing.

"Boy, I asked you a question!" he shouted at me.

I began to grin, showing my teeth and looking all around, as if I was a complete fool. The crowd had grown. They were all laughing at the sheriff.

"Boy! I ain't gonna ask you again, who are you and what are you doing in Keller Point?" I continued to stand there - showing my teeth, smiling, and looking all around.

"I warned ya, boy," the Sheriff said, as he whipped out his pistol and swung at my head.

I ducked and he tripped over the bottom step and sprawled out spread eagle right in front of the laughing crowd. I didn't know what to do so I just stood there. The sheriff grabbed for his pistol, (he had dropped it in the dirt when he fell), and shot me - just grazing my left arm. At lightning speed, I drew and centered a slug right between his eyes.

"Now that is what I call disturbing the peace." You could have heard a pin drop as everyone began to walk away.

After everyone had left, I stepped up on the porch and went inside the shoe repair shop. The clerk was standing behind the counter.

"I know why you're here," he said, leaning over the counter, as if he had something to say to me.

"You don't even know who I am, mister, how can you say that?" I took the two buttons out of my shirt pocket and laid them on the counter in front of him.

"Are you a Texas Ranger?" he asked.

"No, he will be here tomorrow," I answered.

"It is about the young girl, isn't it?" he asked, picking up one of the buttons and giving it close attention.

"Yes, and now the sheriff is dead," I said as I leaned upon the counter, "now why don't you tell me what you know? I asked.

It was like a peace came over him.

"I was inside working when it all took place, outside. I was putting a heel back on a boot that belongs to the girl's best friend, I think I was told."

"That's right, it was Susie that had the boot, and Ruby that got killed."

"I don't know if you noticed the chair sitting out there on the board walk in front of my shop."

"Yes, now that you mention it...I remember it sitting there what has it got to do with the girl getting shot?" I asked.

"Nothing at all, really, but the old man that usually sits out there must have heard it all. 'Course now, I haven't seen him since the girl got shot; which leads me to believe he seen and heard more than he is letting on. I'm sure he seen and heard everything. If you want to talk to him, he lives with his daughter just outside of town and stays broke and drunk most of the time. He goes by Festus when he is sober, and 'the town drunk' when he is three sheets in the wind."

"I think I'll pay him a visit. Just how do I find his house?"

"You'll find it isn't much of a house - there are hog pens built all way around it - and if he is there, he'll be sitting out in the front yard around a passel of hound dogs."

I thanked the man and started out of his shop.

"Don't forget your buttons."

I turned and went back to the counter and picked up the buttons and said, "By the way, my name is Bill Allen. I'm with the wagon train that came through the day the girl was shot, but I was miles away on business."

"My name is Joe Sullivan. I moved here from Ohio about a year ago."

I put the buttons back in my shirt pocket, and made my way out to where my horse was tied. There were two men helping the undertaker load the sheriff up in a hearse. No one said a word, so I mounted up. At the saloon I pulled up to the hitching rail, dismounted, walked up to the bat-wings, and looked inside. It was as empty as last year's bird's nest; the bartender was standing behind the hardwood bar polishing shot glasses.

I didn't seem to surprise him in the least, he never broke stride and went right on polishing glasses.

"Gimme two bottles of your best whiskey, Bartender, the best you have got in the house."

He put both hands on the bar and stepped back, looking me up and down.

"You got any money mister?" the bartender asked, still eyeballing my dirty clothes. I got to admit, I was a sight for sore eyes after crawling under the porch of the shoe repair shop. I reached in the pocket of my dirty Levis and pulled out a roll of bills that would choke a Billy goat, first bite.

"Let me get it for you, Sir, my best is locked up." He quickly turned, taking a key from his neck, and eased over to a cabinet behind the bar, sitting directly under the big picture of the half naked lady. I stood watching as he retrieved two fancy bottles of whiskey from the cabinet and set then on the bar right in front of me.

"You planning on getting inebriated today?" he asked, pulling out his rag and wiping the bar around the two fancy bottles.

"No, I never touch the stuff, it's for a friend," I explained.

"How much do I owe ya?" I asked, picking up the roll of bills.

"Eight dollars..." the bartender said, smiling, "I wish I had a friend like you."

I fumbled through the wad of bills; the smallest I had was a twenty. I slid it across the bar toward the bartender. "Keep the change, mister."

I picked up the bottles and walked out. I slid the two bottles into saddlebag and mounted up, heading down to the hog pen. Not only did I see where Festus lived, but I could smell the stench a city block away. The shoe repairman was right, there he sat in a circle of hound dogs. These dogs were so poor they would have to lean up against the house to bark. I dismounted and started across the yard, shooing the chickens out of my way as I walked.

Chapter Twenty-four

"Can I help you there, Mister?" came a voice from beside the shack. I turned to see a woman behind a number three wash tub leaning over a rub-board.

"I came to see Festus."

"Well you found 'em, he ain't doing so well today." the woman said, wiping her hands on her apron, walking my way.

"What's that you're totin', Mister?"

"I brought Festus a fine bottle of sipping whiskey."

"My pa don't sip whiskey, Mister, he guzzles it. And that's what is wrong with him; he ain't had a drink in a while. He was telling me he seen something in town that had really upset him."

"You don't mind me talking to him, do you?"

"Oh no! Just go on over and kick some of them dogs out of the way, and wave that whiskey bottle under his nose. You can go ahead and pull up that apple box and have a seat."

I guess ol' Festus' daughter had her pa pegged. The waving of the whiskey did the trick. He opened his eyes and pushed his straw hat back on his head, and began to stare me down.

"I brung you a little something to wet your whistle, Mr. Festus," I said, passing him the bottle.

There was no twisting of his arm to get him to drink, his daughter was right; he was chug-a-lugging and nearly half the bottle was gone. He snorted loudly, and shook all over. I stood their watchin' as he wiped his mouth on his sleeve.

"Mister, that's the best drank of whiskey I have ever tasted in my whole life, bar none."

"Well, Mr. Festus, there is plenty more from where that bottle comes from; I got another whole fifth in my saddlebag."

"You don't say?" He turned the bottle up and took a snort and capped the bottle. "Them Turner brothers didn't sends you out here to kill me, did they?" Festus asked, wiping his mouth on the back of his hand.

"No they didn't, but I would like to ask you a few questions." He started shaking his head, as if to say no.

I knew then that he had been threatened by the Turner brothers.

"Do you think they will come over here and harm you?"

"Yes, I do, them or the sheriff."

"You need not worry about the sheriff. I killed him before I come over here to see you."

I reckon the daughter heard me telling Festus I had killed the sheriff and she came over where we were sitting drying her hands.

"Pa, you go ahead and tell the man what he wants to know. You are here about the girl getting shot, aren't you?" she asked.

"Yes, I am, she was a dear friend of mine and was several months with child."

Festus unplugged the bottle and took a big swig. "I'm sure Joe Sullivan sent you out here to talk to me about the girl getting killed." I nodded and grunted, and he went on with his story. "I was sitting on the porch at the shoe repair shop, where I spend most of my time these days. I seen two pretty girls ride up. I watched as they dismounted and tied up there mounts to the hitching rail. They seemed to not be in a hurry as they started inside the shop. The one girl, toting a pair of boots, went on in the shoe shop and the other girl stopped, not more than a few feet from me, and started looking at a pair of fancy boots that Joe had placed in the display window for sale." Festus took him another drink and capped the bottle. He cleared his throat and spit.

"Well, as the devil would have it, here came Ben Turner and his brother Gladden, walking down the boardwalk toward us. I could tell they had been in the saloon, especially Ben; he was loud, and weaving all over the place. Well, when he got right even with the young girl looking at the fancy boots, he stopped and started talking to her."

"Do you remember anything that was said between the two?" I asked, hoping he could shed some light on the torn blouse.

"Yeah, I remember everything that was said, maybe not word for word, but I believe you will know what was said. When Ben Turner got right even with the girl he stopped, and his brother Gladden walked on a ways up the walkway. I remember him stopping and turning around, and he said: 'Come on Ben, and leave the girl alone.' Ben Turner caught hold of the girl and pulled her around facing him and said: 'Hello darling, I haven't seen you around town before'... and she pulled loose and said: 'You get your grubby hands off me'. 'Now, now', he said, 'you don't need to be like that sweetheart, you such a pretty little thing, let ole Ben show you something', and he caught hold of the front of her blouse and staggered back, tearing her blouse. This is when she pulled her pistol...'Let me show you something'. I don't think for one minute she would have shot ole Ben. But call it pride, or lack of good judgment, or making fun of the girl, he took out his pistol and went to waving it around. This is when I got up and got out of the way. Everyone could see he was drunk or he would have never drawn his pistol. I guess the girl got fed up, and shot the pistol out of ole Ben's hand, and started in the shoe repair shop. This is when Gladden drew, and shot the girl three times in the chest."

"Mr. Festus, Gladden Turner didn't just kill a young girl that deserved to live, but killed a baby inside of her. Where would a person find the Turner brothers this time of day?"

"Well, sir, if they ain't out of town robbing a stagecoach, they should be in the saloon by now."

"Now, Festus, that's a strong statement, and it could sure get you into serious trouble. Can you prove it?"

"Yes I can prove it, neither Ben nor Gladden has a job, but they live high on the hog, and the sheriff is, or was, as crooked as they were."

"That may all be true, but that ain't enough of evidence to prove that they rob stages," I said.

"Well how about this, my brother rides shotgun for the stage line and three times he has recognized the brands on their horses, as they held up the stage."

"Why hasn't he said something?" I asked.

"He has a wife and family, and wants to live." I just shook my head and looked over at his daughter.

"You are having a hard time of it, ain't you?"

She nodded and hung her head and replied, "We can't get

anymore credit at the general store."

"How much do you owe the store?" I asked.

"Mr. Grimes said I owed him over sixty dollars, and no more credit until we pay up."

I reached in my pocket and pulled out my roll of bills. "How would you and your pa like to go to work for me?"

She looked at my wad of money, and then asked her pa, "What do you think?"

"It sure isn't any living raisin hogs around here. I'm game if you are. What do you want us to do, Mister?"

"First of all, my name is Bill Allen, and I want you and your daughter to come with me to Fort Worth and run a hog farm for me. I'll build you a nice house to dwell in and pay you both a salary each month."

"That all sounds good, sir. My name is Doris Joiner and I been married before; my husband got killed. What will we do with this place and all these hogs and dogs?"

"Beings you asked, you and your pa needs to take a loss for the land and hogs. Lets us find an overland supply wagon. We'll enlarge the bed so we can bring as many brood sows, as possible, with you when you come to Fort Worth. I would use that buckboard setting over there to bring as much feed as you need to hold the sows over, until we can get a pen built on your ranch. Make up some fliers and post them all over town, that the place is up for sale. Don't turn down a reasonable offer." I could tell my plan brought new life into this couple.

"You know, Bill, I think I'm gonna turn over a new leaf and quit getting drunk, as of right now."

"That's a great idea! What am I going to do with that full bottle in my saddlebag over there on my horse?"

"I think I'll use it for medicine or sipping now and then." We all had a good laugh.

"If you have a place I can brush off and wash up; and you can find a horse that goes with that buckboard settin' over there, I'll carry you and your dad out to dinner tonight," I offered,

"Pa, that's a first for me, my husband never carried me to a café, God rest his stingy soul. You go and get ready. I'll go find the horse and harness him to the wagon."

It wasn't long until we were pulling up to the only café in Keller Point, Texas. The place didn't look all that good from the outside, but

I learned a long ago - don't judge a book by its cover. The food really smelled great, as we went in. The waitress showed us to a table and we took our seat. She disappeared for a minute, but quickly returned with a glasses of water and a menu. She stood with her pencil and pad, and waited.

"What about your steaks, here?" I asked.

"Big and tender, is that what you want?"

"Well, I don't know, let me ask my guests. Will y'all settle for a big, tender steak and all the trimmings, this evening?"

"Right now I would settle for a dish rag with possum gravy on it; I ain't had no solid food in so long, my belly thinks I got lockjaw," Doris said, licking her lips.

"Okay young lady, I guess we are ready to order, give us three of your biggest steaks, and all the trimmings." After the waitress brought the steak I knew right then they were as good with a knife and fork, as I was with a Navy Colt revolver.

"Do y'all think we can eat and talk at the same time?"

"You better believe it," Doris said. "You talk, and we'll be eating."

"You and your pa listen. I've got two men on my wagon train that plan to open up a meat packing and pressing plant when we get set up in Fort Worth. Now I'm sure we can get all the beef we need, but pork, I'm not sure of; that's where you and Doris come in. First of all, I'm not planning on you two working yourself to death; you can hire men to do the labor. I want you two just to see that it is did right, any questions?"

The two were about through with their steaks. What was that old English poem - 'Betwixt and between, they lick the platter clean'? The young lady saw that we were finishing up, and sashayed back with her pad and pencil.

"Can I get something else for y'all?" she asked, smiling from ear to ear.

I wiped my mouth and hands and made eye contact with the young lady. "What do y'all have for dessert?" I asked.

"We have apple pie and bread pudding." I looked over at Doris and Festus. Simultaneously I heard apple pie mentioned.

"Three apple pies and a coffee refill," I told the waitress. She spun around and skipped off toward the kitchen.

Festus tapped me on the back of my hand with a spoon. I turned and caught his gaze as he asked, "Do you know those two men that just walked in?"

I turned and looked toward the front door of the café. There stood two rough looking customers, both wearing a hog leg tied down. "No, I have never seen them in my life; do I suppose to know them?" I asked. I could tell Festus was getting nervous.

"That's the Turner Brothers, Ben and Gladden; they have come to kill me, I bet you anything."

I thought, they have got to kill me first. They came walking over our way about the time the waitress brought the pie and coffee pot.

"Old Festus sitting here tells me you fellows are the famous Turner Brothers."

"And you have got to be the famous sheriff killer. Sheriff Dobbs was our friend, and we are gonna kill you."

I cleared my throat and looked at the two men. They were standing with their feet wide apart and their hands resting on the butt of their pistols.

"Can I finish my apple pie and cup of coffee first?" I asked, as I picked up my fork.

They both looked at each other and laughed. "It ain't no use blooding up the floor in here where folks are trying to eat supper, is it, Gladden?"

"That's right Ben, It ain't no use blooding up the floor; there is plenty of room out in the street."

"I appreciate you girl shooters giving me time to eat my pie and pay my bill, before I die."

"You have said enough boy, we'll be waiting for you outside. When you clear the front door we're going to cut you down, just like you did our friend, Sheriff Dobbs."

"I'm so sorry about that boys, he won't be able to help you assholes rob anymore stagecoaches."

Gladden reached for his gun.

"No! No! Brother," Ben said, putting his hand in front of Gladden, "let him eat his pie, and enjoy his last meal." They both turned, still laughing, and walked to the front door.

"We'll be waiting," was the last word I ever heard them say.

"What's the matter?" I asked, looking over at Doris and Festus, "you ain't gonna eat your pie?"

"Bill, I think you said that was your name, we just lost our appetite," Doris said, laying her fork down beside her plate. "What hopes Dad and I had about going to Fort Worth with you!"

I jumped up and pushed my pie back on the table. "Let me go

and pay our bill and I'll be back to eat my pie." I quickly walked to the counter and gave the girl a fifty dollar bill, "Keep the change," I said, then asked, " do y'all have a back door to this place?"

"Thank you so much, mister," she replied, and pointed to the kitchen part of the café.

I had no trouble finding the back door; I learned long ago to follow my nose and it would take me anywhere I wanted to go. I flipped the thong off the hammer of my Colt and started around the side of the café. It was evening, but there was plenty light to kill two snakes. Sure enough there they stood, with there eyes glued to the front door of the café. As a matter of fact, they never even noticed me when I came around the building. It wasn't going to be a fair fight, they both were holding their pistols in their hands. I went ahead drew my Colt from the holster and held the trigger back, getting ready to start fanning.

"I'm over here!" I yelled. Now as far as I know, I never heard a shot fired other than my own six shots. I guess it surprised everyone when I opened the front door of the café and stepped inside, holding a still smoking Navy Colt. I made my way over to the table where Doris and Festus were both trembling, like a Chihuahua trying to pass a Georgia peach seed.

"I think I'll eat my pie now."

Chapter Twenty-five

The next morning Doris and Festus met me back at the café for breakfast, and we got an early start looking for a wagon for Fetus to haul his brood sows to Fort Worth. We soon found what we were looking for, and at a bargain price, I might add. The wagon needed some minor repair, but it was nothing Fetus couldn't get under control. I also found Fetus was once a smart man, but he, like many, let the bottle get control of his life, after his wife died at an early age.

We also made a covered wagon out of the buckboard by using some slender green saplings to stretch the canvas over. Things were beginning to shape up; Doris even had several offers on the house and property. When the word got out, Fetus even sold most of his hogs, except for the ones he was going to load and carry with him. I spent another night in the local hotel and was ready to leave the next day. I was ready to catch up with my wagon train.

As they say: 'back in the saddle again'. I had reduced the population in Keller Point, Texas; and it didn't seem to bother anyone. Their sentiments, I gathered, before I left was 'Gone and good riddance'. As I got might near out of town, I passed a graveyard and a hearse sitting close by. I saw a rather tall man in a black suit, favoring Abe Lincoln, especially the tall hat. I turned my horse and rode up to where he was standing.

"Good morning to you, sir." I said, sliding around in the saddle.

"And a pleasant morning, to you my good man," he answered, looking me over right closely.

Just over to my left was a fresh grave.

"Do you happen to know who is buried in that new grave?" I asked as I pointed.

"I'm not good in remembering names, but it's right here in my book." Before I had time to tell him not to worry about it. He reached around in the hearse and took out a folder of some sort, favoring a ledger. He pushed his spectacles up on his nose. "It says she was Ruby Mills, age eighteen; to young to die the way she did, if you ask me." He carefully placed the folder back in the hearse.

"I just suppose you bury lots of young folks out here."

"That I do, sir; I buried her right close to my twin daughters." I guess he could see the expression of curiosity on my face, as I dismounted. He began to tell me how they died. "The wife and I had sent the two girls back east for a good education." The gentleman sort of cocked his head placing his finger to his jaw, his eyes glistened, trying to form a tear. "That was over five years ago and I'm still not over it. It was in their first semester the girls took sick." He turned and caught my gaze. "As did over half the college." He paused and walked around the hearse, and looked across the grave yard. "It was some type of epidemic that spread like wild fire. It was about the time of the start of the Civil War back east...no one ever knew what caused it."

"I'm so sorry to hear that, sir. That's a fine tombstone to remember them by." I made a few steps in his direction and asked, "I was just wondering if you sell head markers?"

"Well, yes I do, what did you have in mind?" he asked.

"I want something for the girl's grave right there. What can I get for fifty dollars?"

"For fifty dollars you can a right nice marble tombstone with her name on it."

"What can I get for a hundred dollars?" I prodded.

"Oh well now, you could get something like on my daughters' graves, with name and writing." I pulled my wad of bills out of my Levi's, peeled off a one hundred dollar bill, and took a step and handed it to the man with the tall hat.

"Could I ask you a question, Sir; do you know where they are going to bury Ben and Gladden Tuner?"

"Well yes, I do, that is why I'm out here now, waiting for the two grave diggers. I personally need to show them where to dig the graves. Why do you ask?"

"It's a long story, but I'll put it in a nutshell, the two polecats you are digging the grave for is the two that killed Ruby Mils, the girl that is buried next to your two daughters."

"Well I just do declare! You are saying don't bury the Turner Brothers close to Ruby Mill's grave site?"

"Yes, that is what I'm saying, and I will appreciate it. I do have respect for the dead, even after they are buried. One more thing, if you have your pencil handy, I would like to put on Ruby Mill's headstone: 'I carried my baby to heaven with me', could you do that?" he nodded yes, and tried to swallow.

I thought as I rode off, I'm gonna come back along this way one day and visit Ruby's grave.

With fast riding and one more night sleeping on the ground, I saw the dust of my wagon train ahead. They were just a few days outside of Fort Worth, Texas when I caught up to them. Was I tired! But I had much to tell. At supper I pretty much took the floor, as they say. I told them the goings on, and what happened in Keller Point while I was there, and about having a grave-marker put on Ruby's grave. I was excited telling about Doris and her dad, Festus, bringing a load of breed sows with them to start a hog farm.

Things went well for us the next few days. The men folks and I had several meetings after supper, sitting around the camp fire sipping our coffee.

"What do you men think about us settling down just west of Fort Worth, if we ever get there?" Arthur asked.

"Sounds good to me. I have read much about Fort Worth having plenty of room to homestead. The city was established in 1849 as an Army outpost, on a bluff overlooking the Trinity River.

"As you all know, I plan to build a church, and farm for my living," said Mr. Hicks, adding his approval.

"As for me, I plan to set up my sawmill and go to work; that is if I can find some help," Jeremiah explained.

"As you know, my problem I have got rid of, and I'm just looking for a job when I put down stakes," said Jessie.

"Me and Mary plan to homestead as much land as we can, and start a ranch. I understand Texas longhorns roam the plains and hills grazing, free for the taking, ready to be branded," I said.

"I believe Bill and Mary have the right idea, especially since the railroad is coming to Fort Worth." said Mr. Hicks.

It seemed we were all in one accord about settling down just west of Fort Worth, Texas. So we set our sights on Fort Worth and kept rolling west the next two days.

The abundance of longhorn cattle in south Texas and the return of Confederate soldiers to a poor reconstruction economy marked the beginning of the era of Texas trail drives to northern markets. Finally, this was also the history of the Native Americans who were displaced by these forts and the communities that sprang up around them. The chronicles of the Comanche, Kiowa, and Apache, and Kickapoo tribes are intertwined with these forts; for these posts marked the end of the American Indian way of life, and forever changed their tribal culture. Of course, this didn't set well with the Indians taking their land and killing the buffalo. This was a gold mine for us, selling beeves and horses to the army. The government was buying cattle and giving to the Indians; we were also shipping cattle back east, the five years of civil war had depleted all cattle and horses. The black folks still had a few hogs left when the dust and smoke settle.

As we each signed up for the free homestead land, the transition went well. The only exception was the ranchers that had come earlier thought they had dibs on the land we had just homesteaded. And the mavericks on our land that weren't branded, were our cattle, by law. Now since there was no law out here, the gun spoke louder than words, and that in itself did cause a few problems.

As far as timber was concerned, I believe Jeremiah had the cream of the crop. He had his sawmill up and running, and was selling lumber to beat the band. Seemed that everyone coming west was looking for a job, and Jeremiah had no trouble keeping good help. I can say one thing...Fort Worth, Texas was growing by leaps and bounds; and so was my ranch and herd of longhorns. Our makeshift house wasn't what we wanted, but it would serve me and Mary well for this winter. We had installed two wind mills on our spread, plus we had a small stream going through our property.

I had Susie and Gloria working for me on the ranch. They were doing everything a cowboy could do: marking and branding. They had turned out to be regular cowgirls, and seemed to love the wide open spaces. I helped Mr. Hicks build his church and get his garden started. Arthur had built a right nice house on his homestead spread for Grace and the two children, Jill and Garry.

Festus and Doris had a hog ranch going, second to none. And Marvin and Doug was buying all the pork they could produce. Their smoked hams and shoulders were the best in the west. They stayed sold out of salted side meat and bacon.

Every sunrise was a challenge; Arthur said it looked like we jumped out of the frying pan into the fire. We had trouble with the Comanche, Kiowa, Apache, and Kickapoo tribes, not to mention the ornery carpetbaggers, poachers, squatters, sod busters and sheep herders. And then, the cattle rustlers and outlaws tried to take over.

It just seemed that killing and people wanting what wasn't theirs, was the order of the day. I guess the stage lines were hit the hardest; it was near impossible for gold coming from California to get back east. The Pinkerton Agents had developed another side of the law with their distasteful reputation. The Texas Rangers were making waves across the Long Horn State by bringing law and order, and I might say it was about time.

One could say, and I would agree, that the new saloon in town was causing more deaths than stage holdups, bank robberies, or gun fights on Main Street. It was a known fact that the drovers enjoyed their fun after a month or so on a trail drive. Don't say I said it, but they would get all liquored up and shoot their own brother over a bar-room whore.

Sheriffs came and went in Fort Worth like seasons of the year; there wasn't a graveyard around here without a sheriff or two planted in it. Boot hills were popping up all over the place. So were more dance halls, gambling joints, and saloons. Of course, the undertaker and gunsmiths had their hands full.

I guess you want to know...Me and Mary finally tied the knot and were waiting on a baby to come; I had ordered a white-faced Hereford bull from back east, and didn't know which would get here first. Susie and Gloria worked along with two drifters I hired that had come along looking for a cow punching job. As the story goes, here's how the first trouble started: The girls and the two drifters had rounded up twenty five or thirty head of longhorns and penned them up to be marked and branded. We were all hotter than a Henry barrel at a turkey shoot, when these three riders rode up. The first thing I noticed was they didn't look like cowpokes, or the run of the mill cowboys. All three were riding fine mounts and had a Colt hanging low on their hip, tied to their legs. Seems my crew had everything under control, so I excused myself and walked over to the corral fence where the strangers were staring us down. I leaned over the top board, placing one boot on the bottom.

"Can I help you gentlemen this fine morning?" I asked, knowing full well these gunslingers weren't here to discuss the weather.

"Did you know that cattle rustling don't set well with Mr. Cole?" one of the men announced, as if he had some authority to do so.

"Don't set well with me either, and who is this Mr. Cole character you speak of?"

The spokesman of the trio turned and looked at the other two sitting there smiling as if they had chomped into a green persimmon. "He don't know who Mr. Cole is, can y'all believe that?" the big man blurted out. I stood shaking my head as the men looked on.

"I know who George Washington and Abraham Lincoln are, and even who the Pope is...but this Cole you speak of is not in my head."

I could tell this conversation was about over, I saw the look in their eyes.

"Just one minute before you ride off, my girls may know who Mr. Cole is, they do get around." I backed away from the fence and called Susie and Gloria, "Come over here and tell these gentlemen if you know Mr. Cole."

I don't think our three strangers noticed when Gloria and Susie flipped the thong off their Colts as they were getting up from branding a critter. I knew that they weren't watching me remove the thong from my Navy Colt. The two girls with their tight pants came prancing across the corral lot, swinging their hips from side to side. I knew by the way they stopped and positioned themselves, they knew I needed help. I also knew that the person standing on solid ground had the advantage over a man sitting a horse...because at the sound of the first shot the horses would spook.

"Do either of you ladies know the Mr. Cole the nice gentlemen are referring to?"

"Is he tall and handsome. with a mustache?" asked Susie.

"No, Susie, I think he is the short one. and wears a white suit."

"Look...! Y'all don't know who Mr. Cole is, but he hired us to do a job, let's get it over, fellas." I saw his arm move, going for his pistol,. and that was the last word he spoke on this green earth. I could feel the wind, slam over where I stood. Susie and Gloria were fanning their Colts as if they were putting out a wild fire. It still amazes me, those girls can do more tricks with a six shot revolver than a monkey can do on a hundred foot of grape vine.

Chapter Twenty-six

When the smoke and the dust settled, we all walked out of the corral where the three men lay, with there pistols still in their holsters.

"Jake catch up with their horses and put them in the corral by the barn; go ahead and unsaddle them and throw the tack in the barn. Les, you go and bring the buckboard. I'm going to let you haul these buzzards into town. Susie, you and Gloria see who you sent to hell. And while you're at it, strip them of their gun rigging."

The first man Susie rolled over was carrying a roll of bills. "Look at this Boss Man!" She walked over where I was standing. "There is more than five hundred dollars here."

"You and Gloria just go ahead and split it, how much does that man have, Gloria?" She unfastened his gun belt, untied it from his leg, pulled it out from under him and took out his billfold.

"About the same amount, I'll check the third man," said Gloria. She took off his gun and holster then checked his billfold. "He has a wad also. This must be the money they were paid for making short order of us," she reported.

"As I said, you girls split the money. And thanks a bunch."

I guess Mary heard the shooting down at the ranch house and here she came trying to run, but she was big as a barrel with our baby. Out of breath she asked, "What was all the shooting about?" before she saw the three men lying on the ground.

Susie was the closest, and replied. "It seems for all I can make out, this ole man hired these three gunslingers to come over here and stop our operation."

"Why do you suppose he'd do a fool thing like that?" Mary asked, holding her stomach. Gloria walked over and joined in on the conversation.

"I don't know if Susie heard this or not, but one of the men accused Mr. Bill of rustling his cows."

Well, Mary was just put out with the news of more killing, and knew this would not be the last. And she was right. After Les and Jake took the three dead men to the undertaker, it didn't just open up a can of worms...it literally turned over a keg of snakes.

This "Cole" name grew more popular as the days grew longer. It didn't take us long to find out he had a ranch north of Fort Worth, and we little ranchers were infringing on his cows. As it was, this Cole character had come from Boston and homesteaded a ranch a year before we arrived. Evidently he didn't pay much attention to where his boundaries were. It was plain to see that Cole had skimmed the rich cream from the top and sent cows back east without being branded. 'Course now he thought we small ranchers were intruding on his property and cows.

I knew where my boundaries were, and had only branded cows and horses on the land I had a claim on. I found out from a very reliable source in town, old man Cole's wife had left him and gone back east to Boston. Seems she was a good Methodist, and didn't go along with her husband's shenanigans: cheating, lying and running good folks off their farms and ranches. This within itself caused bitterness and an attitude problem. This is where money overshadowed his sense of honesty. He had become rich and the cattle on his land were drying up. Mr. Cole was blaming his dwindling fortune and loss of his rich lifestyle on everyone but himself.

Gunslingers around Fort Worth were a dime a dozen, they were looking for work without having to work. Little farmers and ranchers like me were easy prey for the already rich and famous. But if they thought I would turn tail and run...they had another thought coming.

Fort Worth went from a sleepy outpost to a bustling town when it became a stop along the legendary of the Chisholm Trail, the dusty path on which millions of head of cattle were driven north to market. Fort Worth became the center of the cattle drives, and later, the ranching industry. It's location on the Old Chisholm Trail helped establish Fort Worth as a trading and cattle center and earned it the nickname "Cow town."

The railroad to Fort Worth took the place of the stagecoach. and put the icing on the cake. Oh yes, the baby came, and so did my white-faced Hereford bull. Now Mary and I have a ranch house full of children, and miles of white-faced Hereford cattle. Who says a Georgia boy and a girl from Alabama can't tame the Wild, Wild West.

The End

Other Great Books By Charlie Barnett

Amazing Grace

Cat man Road

Dead But Not Buried

Devils, Daemons And Deliverance

Georgia Cowboy

Going Back To Abilene

Go West Young Man

Heading West

Humorous Poems & Funny Stories

I Fell In Love With My Rapist

Just Jokes

My Mother Was An Angel

Run Johnny Run

Short Stories Told By My Granny

Standing In The Shadow

Suitcase Full Of Money

Through The Bible In Poems

Youngest Gun Slinger

Heading West

Website: www.gateswoodbooks.com

About The Author

Born in 1936, Charlie Barnett has lived his whole life within three acres of where he first saw the light of day. At the age of thirteen, Charlie began publishing a monthly school comic book. Today, 62 years later, he has authored sixteen books with many more on the way. Charlie has also penned over 200 poems that range from inspirational to southern humor.

Before retiring, Charlie spent decades as a successful entrepreneur and minister. He enjoys writing, watching westerns, gardening, and observing butterflies and hummingbirds.

Charlie has been married to his wife, Janice, since 1958. Today they enjoy their growing family that includes four sons, eleven grandchildren and eight great-grandchildren. Charlie is always up for a good laugh, telling stories, and speaking engagements.

Visit Charlie on the web at www.gateswoodbooks.com

www.ingramcontent.com/pod-product-compliance
Lightning Source LLC
Chambersburg PA
CBHW060109260626
47160CB00005B/1841